Dear Readers,

**T4-BAG-168**

We've made a New Year's resolution—to bring you the best in contemporary romance. Why not make a resolution of your own and treat yourself to a Bouquet today?

This month, Zebra, Bantam, and Love Spell author Kate Holmes takes readers to a windswept North Carolina beach, where a shy artist and a world-weary photographer take the first steps toward love as they build **Sand Castles** . . . and a beautiful future together. From veteran Zebra author Clara Wimberley comes **Beneath A Texas Moon,** a poignant story of one woman's second chance at love with the man who taught her about passion—a man who's about to learn he's the father of her child.

On the lighter side, **Dangerous Moves** is Mary Jane Morgan's look at how opposites attract, in which a thrill-seeking cowboy decides to take his pretty physical therapist for the ride of her life . . . for good. Finally, beloved, prize-winning author Deb Stover presents **A Matter of Trust,** the story of a young doctor returning to her small hometown to discover that the high school sweetheart who broke her heart is still around—and eager to make amends meet in the sweetest way.

So start your New Year off right . . . with four breathtaking new love stories from Bouquet.

Kate Duffy
Editorial Director

# A MATTER OF TRUST

Gordon closed the door behind her and walked woodenly to the bed. He wanted to forgive Taylor. Desperately. But he couldn't trust her.

If he allowed himself to trust her, she'd have the power to hurt him. No matter what, he couldn't give her that power ever again.

The floor creaked just beyond Gordon's door, and he held his breath as the doorknob turned. His heart thundered in his chest and he wanted desperately to call out to her.

Slowly, the door opened, and Taylor stood framed by firelight.

*Dear God.* His gaze drifted down the length of her, savoring every inch of bare leg. His body sprang to life, even as his mouth formed the words. "Taylor, don't . . ."

"I've been lying awake, and I can't stop remembering." She padded barefoot to his bed. "Look at me, Gordon."

He raised his lashes and met her gaze. Something bright and hot and dangerous burned in her eyes. "Do you know . . ."

She put her knee on his bed and cupped his cheek with one hand, then brought her other knee onto his bed and framed his face with both hands. "I only know this," she whispered, leaning closer to cover his mouth with hers.

Gordon held his breath as she pulled him closer, stroking his lips with her tongue until he growled and wrapped his arms around her to tug her down on top of him.

He should hate her. He should fight this.

He couldn't.

Gordon lost himself in their kiss. . . .

# A MATTER OF TRUST

## DEB STOVER

Zebra Books
Kensington Publishing Corp.

http://www.zebrabooks.com

*This book is for my Genie RomEx Sisters, who've encouraged and supported me through the good and the bad—especially Anne Stuart, Barbara Samuel, Jo Beverley, Karen Harbaugh, Rosalyn Alsobrook, Judith Arnold, Susan Wiggs, and Susan Shwartz.*
*RomEx Rules!*

*And thanks to the WYRD Sisters,*
*who always make me do it right.*

# ONE

Gordon Lane climbed from the frigid mountain stream and looked for his towel.

It was gone. Again.

"You worthless, fur-covered sack of manure," he grumbled, clambering up the bank to the trail, noticing the dumb grin on his aging Irish setter's mug. "Why don't you ever bark at him, Max?" Of course, Gordon knew the answer—the dog was half blind and half deaf.

The dog didn't answer, so Gordon turned his attention uphill again toward his invisible nemesis. "Well, at least you left my boxers. *Real* decent of you."

To say he was angry would be the understatement of the century. Unfortunately, to say he was freezing his family jewels off would be the gospel truth.

He glanced down, half expecting to find icicles affixed to his anatomy. So far, so good. Scowling toward the trees above the stream, he shook his fist. "I swear there's going to be bear stew for dinner; then I'm going to turn what's left of you into a rug for Max."

The bear—aka practical joker in residence—didn't belong to anyone. He came with the property.

Though Gordon had never actually seen him, the evidence the klutzy animal always left in his wake was proof enough. The realtor should have listed the beast as a permanent fixture.

Cocking his head at an angle, Gordon listened to an unexpected—and unwelcome—sound. A car. And instead of turning around at the dead end, the intruder stopped in front of his cabin. *Great. Perfect.*

Putting dry clothes on his wet body wasn't Gordon's favorite way to start the day, but neither was streaking. He hesitated for a moment, mischievous thoughts skipping through his mind. Why not? After all, he hadn't invited anyone.

"Whatcha think, Max?"

The dog's tongue lolled out of the side of his grinning face. "Okay, nah." Gordon tugged on his boxer shorts and decided he'd better get up there before the bear paid a visit. Gordon's breath came out in bursts of white vapor in the morning air as he picked his way barefoot through the trees.

Then something bit him. Up close and *really* personal.

He held his breath and looked down. Dozens of red ants were crawling out of his shorts and all over him, biting again and again.

Howling in pain, he tugged frantically at his waistband. To hell with his company *and* that damned bear. Right now, all he could think about was getting rid of the attack-shorts and cooling the sting.

Which was worse—frozen anatomy or burning?

"Yeow!" An ant bit him in a particularly tender spot.

No contest. Burning.


Taylor Bowen stared in disbelief at the rustic cabin. She must've taken a wrong turn, thanks to a brand-new overpass. One thing was for sure—this wasn't Digby.

She opened her car door and climbed out into the coldest air she'd encountered in ten years. "Brrr. How soon we forget."

The crisp temperature enhanced the fragrance of the pine needles cushioning the ground. She'd missed that fragrance, though she hadn't realized it until now. Awesome beauty mated with the incredible silence and closed in around her, making her feel totally alone.

And vulnerable.

Shifting her gaze from one side of the cabin to the other, Taylor half expected some wild beast to leap out in front of her and make her its breakfast. Hard to believe she'd grown up in these mountains. She slid her sunglasses farther up on her nose and pushed back a strand of dark hair that had escaped from her braid.

Her sweater was blue, so she wasn't in costume for Little Red Riding Hood. No Big Bad Wolf lurked behind the next tree. Of course, that meant there was no grandmother's house at the end of the trail either.

Pulling the front of her sweater closed against the morning chill, she stepped onto the front porch.

Just as she lifted her hand to knock, a bloodcurdling howl shattered the silence.

"What in the world?" She ran down the steps and froze beside her Volkswagen. "A cougar?" A dangerous, wounded animal? She shuddered as the unwelcome memory attacked from all fronts.

"Yeow," came another howl.

"That's no animal." She opened her car door and pulled her leather medical bag from the passenger seat, then ran in the general direction of the sound.

Through the trees, a sparkle of water caught her attention and she hurried, half sliding the last few yards, until the trail took a sharp downward turn. She scanned the area for any sign of life—human or otherwise—then eased herself onto a boulder and looked down.

A man danced down the sloping bank, slapping at his shorts and swearing, while an Irish setter pranced excitedly around him. The man twisted and turned, clearly unaware of his human audience.

He didn't seem hurt. Maybe she should leave before he saw her, saving them both the embarrassment. But as she turned, he howled again; then everything seemed to slip into slow motion. His arms windmilled as he tumbled down the bank and into the water.

Shading her eyes, Taylor ran to the stream just as he dragged himself toward the bank, shaking water from his hair. Her relief that he didn't require rescue barely had time to register before he slumped back against a large flat rock, his lower half still submerged. The Irish setter took position at the man's head, on a flat—and very dry—boulder.

Regardless of the man's bizarre behavior before the fall, Taylor couldn't leave him there. She had to make sure he was all right. Even if he wasn't severely injured, hypothermia could kill him just as thoroughly as drowning. Not taking time to kick off her sandals, she splashed into the pebble-strewn creek.

A quick glance revealed that his eyes were closed as he moaned quietly. *Breathing—okay.* At least that was encouraging, though he obviously hadn't heard her approach over the rushing stream.

A nagging voice in the back of her mind insisted that she look at his face again. Because of his silver hair, she'd thought him a much older man from a distance. Recognition waged a major assault . . . and won.

*Gordon.* Her throat convulsed and her pulse hit the critical level. Suddenly, her need to determine the severity of his injuries became way too personal. He was going to be all right—he had to be.

With shaking hands, she placed her bag on the rock and opened it, wondering how serious his injuries were. After jerking her stethoscope from her medical bag, she moved closer. *Airway, breathing, circulation,* she reminded herself. Her gaze dipped lower to check for bleeding, and she noticed the swirling silver hair covering his torso.

He moaned again and shifted slightly, though his eyes remained closed. "Those bloodthirsty little monsters better be dead, because I'm freezing," he mumbled.

The setter—could it be Max?—barked in agreement.

"D-dead?" she repeated.

Gordon opened one eye to stare at her. "What the—"

Taylor straightened so quickly that she stumbled, barely catching herself before pitching forward. Now *that* would be a great way to start her career. She could already see the headlines:

KLUTZY QUACK KILLS HIGH SCHOOL SWEETHEART

With a groan, he pushed himself to a sitting position. "Between the ants and good Samaritans, a man can't—"

His gaze collided with hers and he blinked several times. "Taylor?"

The dog said, "Woof."

Taylor shook herself from her daze and took a step toward him. "I . . . I thought you were hurt."

"Taylor," he repeated.

His gravelly voice rumbled around in her belly and spiked straight to her bone marrow. *Easy.* She swallowed hard and tried to look away, failing miserably. "Are you hurt? Where are you hurt?"

"You're home." Disbelief filled his voice, reminding her where she was . . . and who *he* was. He rubbed his temples and flashed her a crooked grin. "I'm going to stand up now. You finished playing doctor?"

Taylor tried to ignore the implication of his words and his smile, but she couldn't. They *had* played doctor . . . once upon a time. "I'm not finished checking you yet."

She lifted her chin a notch. This was the first time she'd laid eyes on him since leaving Digby. The relentless pain bypassed her brain and zoomed in on her heart.

With perfect aim.

She didn't need this—not now. Sure, she'd known she would have to face him, but not so soon. Drawing a deep breath, she forced herself to meet his gaze without faltering.

In spite of the bittersweet memories bombarding her, she saw the devil in his turquoise eyes. Gordon's sense of humor hadn't changed a bit, though she suspected it was more of a defense mechanism for him right now. Well, two could play at this game, and it might keep her from turning into a blubbering fool in front of him. She wasn't about to give an inch.

"I'm not finished examining you," she repeated.

"Exa—" He closed his eyes for a moment and released a long, slow breath. "I guess you're a real doctor by now." He gave a nervous chuckle and shook his head. "You know, I didn't recognize you . . . at first." His voice fell to a whisper.

Good thing his injuries weren't serious, because she was doing a pitiful job of maintaining any semblance of professionalism. Not to mention what seeing him again after all this time was doing to the rest of her, especially her heart.

A delicious memory streaked to the forefront of her addled brain, igniting a slow burn through her veins. She saw Gordon as he'd looked more than ten years ago, kissing her, wanting her, baring her virginal flesh to his equally innocent touch. . . .

How she'd wanted him.

A series of images from that long, hot summer between their junior and senior years in high school flashed through her mind—picnics, fishing, hiking, swimming, making out behind the waterfall farther up the mountain and in the backseat of his Jeep. . . .

They'd lost their innocence together. He'd been so tender, so passionate, so . . . Gordon.

The sudden tightening low in her middle jerked her back to the present. She couldn't want him now—not after what he'd done to her. To *them.*

She *wouldn't* want him now. Their relationship was history—a closed chapter in her life. Remembering was sweet but dangerous. It made her vulnerable to the pain—a luxury she couldn't afford. Moistening her lips, she searched his face, wondering if he remembered, too.

He winced as he pushed himself forward.

"You *are* hurt." She took another step toward him. "Is it your back? That was a nasty fall."

"Oh, yeah, I fell. Trust me, you don't want to know about my injuries."

"I think an X—"

"Not necessary." Chuckling, he stood in one smooth movement and wavered only slightly before collecting himself. "See? I'm fine."

Max woofed again. "Is that Max?" she asked in disbelief. "He must be at least twelve by now."

"Thirteen."

Gordon stood so close she could *feel* him, though

she didn't dare lower her gaze. But an insistent voice from some twisted part of her psyche wanted to.

Badly.

Instead, she bit the inside of her cheek and tilted her head back slightly to meet his gaze. Gorgeous eyes, nice tan, long silver hair, and a tall, muscular build—the kind of man women fantasized about.

She ought to know.

He was a grinning bronze god, no longer the acne-prone teenager she'd once loved with all the youthful exuberance she could muster. Or the boy who'd promised his undying love, then had broken her fragile young heart.

"Look, Ma, no hands," he said quietly, continuing to hold her gaze.

Something flickered in the depths of his eyes that momentarily stole her breath. His stare was penetrating, questioning, all-encompassing.

*He remembers, too.* Jerking herself back to reality, she watched him for any hint of instability. "You *did* fall, didn't you?"

"Yeah, sorta, but I definitely had motivation." He looked down at himself. "The water seems to have helped, though."

Without thinking, Taylor followed the direction of his gaze. Wet, clinging boxer shorts—white, of course—left little to the imagination. In addition to his rather impressive physique, angry red welts covered his lower abdomen, inner thighs, and, she suspected, other more intimate areas. "You're . . ."

"Stung," he finished, flashing her another crooked grin when she looked up at his face again.

"Stung," she repeated stupidly, ignoring the voice of feminist reason that told her that she should be offended by her own inability to put two coherent words together. Actually, *magnificent* had been the word floating around in her stunned gray matter.

Little Gordon Lane had matured *nicely*.

Volcanic activity accurately described the inferno that suddenly crept over her. Still, curiosity battled embarrassment and won. "What happened?"

He shrugged. "Ants in my pants." He gestured toward the bank. "Like a fool, I left them on the ground while I went swimming, and wonder dog here never even growled while they invaded."

"I see." She saw, all right—and remembered. Skinny-dipping had been one of their favorite pastimes. Swimming in the buff had been incredibly erotic foreplay. Her memory was too good. Excellent, as a matter of fact.

Forcing her thoughts back into focus, Taylor roused herself and reached behind him for her medical bag. The icy water had numbed her feet and her sandals were ruined. "Well, since you don't want to take my advice and—"

"Nope."

He might as well have said, "Case closed—end of discussion."

He stepped around her, brushing against her arm. The feel of his water-chilled skin seeped through her sweater and straight to her libido. *Good morning, hormones.* Knowing he wore almost nothing didn't help matters any.

A splashing sound prompted Taylor to look over

her shoulder. He was bent over, splashing water onto his abdomen and thighs, oblivious—or indifferent— to the imposing spectacle he presented.

Men's backsides had never commanded her attention before, but now she had to wonder *why*. Lowering her sunglasses, she peered over the rims, then pushed them back into place. Through the thin wet cotton, well-defined muscles rippled along the backs of his thighs and into his buttocks. He was fine. Better than fine, in fact.

Despite her earlier embarrassment, Taylor couldn't prevent the hungry rush that surged through her again. She was a healthy, twenty-eight-year-old woman, after all, and it had been a long, *long* time. Through medical school and residency, her love life had been practically nonexistent. Except for Jeremy—kind, sweet, *safe* . . .

Gordon looked well equipped to satisfy her hunger, but she had other, more pressing matters to consider. Perhaps less appealing, but infinitely more important. Besides, he'd hurt her in the worst possible way. That knowledge stood between her and anything her libido might have in mind.

Brokenhearted, Taylor had told her mother the whole story of Gordon's betrayal. Since her parents were preparing to retire and move to Florida, they decided to send Taylor on ahead to stay with her aunt. Unable to face Gordon, Taylor had made her parents promise not to tell him where she'd gone.

Now she'd come full circle.

Did Gordon know that she knew? Surely he'd realized the reason for her sudden departure.

Dragging in a deep breath, she forced her thoughts away. For now. Later, when she was alone, she knew those memories would return with a vengeance. Well, she'd just have to deal with them.

But first and foremost, she had an obligation to the citizens of Digby. She winced, pushing back the disappointment that again threatened her resolve.

She should be at a large hospital conducting research, not standing in a frigid mountain stream. Sighing, she reminded herself that if not for Digby's financial assistance, she wouldn't have been able to finish medical school at all.

"Enjoying the view?" He straightened and turned to face her in one fluid movement.

Taylor pressed her lips together and purposely allowed her gaze to travel the length of him. Of course, at this point she knew the chances of embarrassing him were nil, but she had to fight back somehow. "Actually, I have better things to do." *In my dreams.* She met his gaze and took a step toward the bank. "Since you won't go to the hospital, at least let me help you back to your cabin."

He cocked an eyebrow and gave her a nod. "Anybody ever call you stubborn as hell?"

"Yeah, you."

He sobered, and she knew he was as haunted by ghosts from the past as she. *Good.* At least there was some justice in the world.

"Well, since we're both heading in the same direction anyway, I suppose there's nothing wrong with letting you come along." He flashed another grin, and Max barked again.

"Fine." She waded from the stream and started up the steep trail, her sodden sandals making loud, squishing sounds. Only the bright sunshine kept her from freezing. This was her first day back in Digby and she hadn't even found the town yet. Oh, yeah, she was really on a roll.

"By the way, thanks," he said, so quietly she almost missed it.

His gratitude surprised her. She should hate him, and she was more than a little surprised to discover she didn't. Well, maturity helped some, she decided.

Right now, the only way out of this mess was to joke her way out of it. It obviously worked as a defense mechanism for him, so why not her?

Pausing on the trail, she smiled to herself. She shouldn't, but she couldn't resist looking over her shoulder and flashing him what she hoped was her most lascivious smile. "I'm sorry. What did you say a while ago?"

He glanced back over his shoulder, a puzzled expression creasing his brow. "Thank you?"

"Ah, that's right." She waggled her eyebrows and allowed her gaze to drift down the length of him. "No. Thank *you*."

He laughed, a rich, vibrant sound that filled the forest and warmed her soul. He'd changed so much—in all the right places—but he was still Gordon.

His laughter ended abruptly and Taylor dragged her gaze from his awe-inspiring body up to his face.

Reminiscing was destroying what remained of her self-control.

His expression said, "If you want it, here it is."

Her body answered from somewhere deep in her core—silently, thank goodness—"Give it to me. Now."

Her gaze dropped again, maddeningly. The ants obviously hadn't inflicted any serious damage. Even through his wet shorts, his arousal was blatant. Impressive.

Compelling.

Taylor swallowed hard and turned to make her way back up the hill, acutely aware that he and Max followed only a few feet behind. As she remembered the sight of him bent over in the stream, a wicked smile tugged at her lips.

She should've let him go first.


Taylor had come home.

Unbelievable but true. Gordon watched the enticing sway of her hips as she climbed the hill in front of him. *Oh, yeah—it's Taylor, all right.*

Why was she here? And, more importantly, why the hell did it matter?

Remembering the last time he'd seen her, he clenched his teeth to silence the string of profanities that filled his mind. She'd walked away from him—from them.

Though she'd sworn to love him forever, she'd cast their love aside without a second thought. Why? Because she hadn't trusted him.

*Old news, Lane.*

He glanced down warily at his still damp boxer shorts. If not for his uninvited guest, he would've removed the shorts . . . just in case. So far, no more bites. His icy extermination had been thorough.

His head throbbed; the ant bites itched and stung. Yes, he needed a little first aid, but he was more than capable of tending his own wounds. His days of playing doctor with Taylor Bowen were long past.

*Taylor.* Why did his angel of mercy have to be the one woman who'd broken his heart? All right, so they'd been teenagers at the time, but that didn't make the memory any less painful.

"A bear!"

Her shout shattered the morning calm as they reached the top of the hill in front of his cabin. In his near-naked splendor, Gordon charged into the clearing and stopped short when he saw the cause of her terror—dozens of huge bear prints.

Max stopped and whimpered.

"Some watchdog you are."

Normally, Gordon would consider Taylor's reaction ridiculous, but he remembered that at the ripe old age of ten, she'd spent several terrified hours cornered by a wounded bear. Her fear was perfectly understandable.

"Damn." He released a long sigh and looked toward her car. "Ah, my towel."

Taylor backed against a tree and dropped her leather bag; her sunglasses fell unheeded to the ground.

Hoping to reassure her, Gordon allowed himself

a small smile. "At least he always returns them. I'd be out a fortune in towels if he didn't."

"A b-bear?"

Gordon glanced at her from the corner of his eye. All color had drained from her face and her eyes were huge as she stared at her car. Max sidled up alongside and looked up at her adoringly.

"The bear's gone now. Besides, he won't hurt you." *I hope.* With a disgusted groan, Gordon walked to her car and retrieved his formerly white towel.

"See, that old bear never lets anyone see him, so he's harmless," he repeated steadily, returning to stand beside her.

When he looked at Taylor again, her eyes grew even larger, though she didn't move or utter a sound. Gordon was pretty sure breathing wasn't high on her current list of priorities either. Max whimpered.

Gordon wanted to touch her—desperately. Why did he still care? After high school, she'd written him off. Correction—written *them* off.

They'd been so much in love.

*Ah, cut the crap, Lane.* He sounded like a lovesick teenager. Whining.

Suddenly, her knees gave and she slid to the ground, her back pressed firmly against the tree. Her face was still white and her hands trembled as she clenched them in front of her. Max licked her cheek and ear, but she didn't even flinch.

Gordon stooped at her side, resisting the urge to cup her face in his hands, to stroke her silky hair away from her eyes. Right now, he was jealous of old Max. "It's all right. The bear's gone now."

She didn't make a sound, but at least she looked up at him again. That was progress.

The sight of her slightly upturned nose with freckles sprinkled across its bridge made his chest tighten. Her full mouth looked too large for her small face. Dark brown curls with a hint of red fell around her face, framing eyes as green as he remembered.

Life couldn't be this cruel.

Holding his breath, he studied her pretty face. *Even prettier now.* Oh, yes, life could be this cruel. It was almost laughable.

Then why wasn't he laughing?

*Enough.* She was frightened and he was taking a stroll down Memory Lane. "You aren't wearing perfume, are you?" he asked, just in case.

The terror in her eyes was very real, but she managed to shake her head.

"Good." He chuckled, hoping to ease her mind. "I haven't seen it for myself, but I've heard that bears have a fondness for perfume. Not a pretty sight, I'm told."

The minute the intended joke left his mouth, he knew he'd made a mistake. He reached for her hands, but before he could touch her, she shot to her feet and sprinted to her car. Intuition told him to run after her, but common sense demanded he disobey.

Besides, she was already in her car and had the engine started. He took a step toward his cabin as she dropped the Bug into gear and sped away, but his foot brushed against something smooth. Glancing down, he saw her leather bag and sunglasses.

"Damn." More memories assaulted him as he slid the sunglasses into the bag and stared at it.

Memories he didn't want.

"Get over it," he muttered, walking toward the house with Max at his heels. Now he'd have to go find her. At least this gave him an excuse—not that he wanted one.

A few feet from the porch, he froze. Suddenly, he knew why she was here—she had to be the new doctor. He'd known about the town's deal with a medical student, but her identity came as a complete surprise. Why would Taylor agree to give three years of her life to Digby?

A barrage of conflicting emotions sliced through him. Joy. Disbelief. Anger.

Why hadn't the mayor revealed the doctor's identity? Then another memory brought a smile to his face. Former Mayor Reynolds had selected the candidate personally. Just before his death, Reynolds had made a remark to Gordon about Tom Bradshaw, Digby's new mayor. It hadn't made sense then, but it sure did now.

*I'd sell my soul to live long enough to see the look on Tom's face the first time he has to bend over and cough for the new doc.*

"That old fart." He drew a deep, cleansing breath, then chuckled. "Taylor." When he'd first opened his eyes and found her looking at him like that, he'd thought maybe he was dead. It could've been heaven—at least, his perception of heaven.

He glanced down at Max. "Was she real, boy?"

"Woof."

"I was afraid of that." Gordon's groin tightened again in recollection, bringing a painful reminder of his close encounter of the insect kind. At least her arrival and his physical response had proven one thing.

Those damned ants hadn't done any permanent damage.

# TWO

After locating the brand-new and confusing over-pass, Taylor drove in circles for nearly an hour before she stumbled across the old, familiar road to Digby. If she'd found it the first time, she could have driven straight into town.

And avoided seeing Gordon.

The way he'd looked at her . . .

"Stop, already." She parked her car, banishing further thoughts of this morning. Of Gordon.

Digby hadn't changed much in ten years. It was almost as if she'd never left. Her stomach clenched. *But I did leave.* For a darned good reason, too. Blinking back the stinging sensation in her eyes, she stooped to retrieve her purse and medical bag, coming up one short.

Realization slammed into her with a definite lack of finesse. "Oh, no." She'd left her bag at Gordon's place.

In her mind, she pictured him again, bent over in the stream. Why couldn't he have acquired a potbelly, or gone bald, or *something* to make him less attractive? His prematurely gray hair only made him sexier.

Not fair.

She'd have to go after the bag later, or maybe she could send someone after it. Yes, that was a much better—safer—idea.

She looked across the street, locating the house immediately. Her parents' old house. When the mayor's secretary told her the place was for rent furnished, Taylor'd asked her to lease it without hesitation. Some wise investor had obviously seen its potential.

Her childhood home. Mom and Dad were happily retired in Florida now, but Taylor's remembrance of this place flooded and warmed her. Smiling, she tilted her head back and gazed up at the restored structure, complete with turrets and gingerbread. The new owner had taken great pains to ensure the historical integrity of the place.

Tall pines and aspen still shaded the back of the house; her mother's favorite rosebush stood in the corner of the yard, loaded with promising pink buds. It was a little early yet for flowers in the high country. She hoped a late frost wouldn't kill them.

Drawing a deep breath, she opened the gate and fished the key from her jeans pocket. She stepped onto the porch, clutching the key in her fist. *Home.*

"Temporarily," she said quietly, allowing herself this one fantasy. For three years this would be home; then she'd apply for every research grant in the nation until she found one. The right one. A shiver raced through her at the thought of unraveling medical mysteries. . . .

Her life's ambition—her dream.

As the door swung open, an insistent pressure filled her chest. Her vision blurred and she blinked again to clear it, refusing to acknowledge the barrage of emotions attacking from all sides.

*It's only temporary, Taylor,* she reminded herself as the screen swung shut behind her.

The house still smelled of lemon oil, just as it always had. A blue overstuffed chair sat near the front window and a small table occupied the room's center.

A gasp tore from her throat when she caught sight of the piano. *Mom's piano.* She dropped her purse and rushed across the room to touch the instrument, remembering the countless hours her mother had played for them.

The phone rang, slicing through her memories, dragging her back to the present. She shook herself and crossed the room to pick up the receiver.

"Hello," she said, then cleared her throat and repeated the greeting.

"Mayor Bradshaw here. Welcome to Digby, Dr. Bowen," a friendly male voice boomed through the receiver.

Taylor held the phone away from her ear slightly. "Thank you."

"I've only been in Digby about five years," he continued. "My secretary told me this is a homecoming for you."

"Well . . ." Taylor shrugged out of her sweater and dropped it over the back of the chair. "It's only temporary."

"I hope you change your mind about that." Several seconds of dead space occupied the phone line;

then he said, "I trust my secretary had the house in order for you."

"Yes, it's lovely."

"Great. I'm sorry I can't say the same about the new clinic."

"Oh?" Alarm bells clanged in Taylor's head. She could see herself practicing medicine right here in the den, just like Marcus Welby.

"Bad weather this spring delayed construction." A loud sigh came through the line. "It's an empty shell right now."

"I see." Taylor mentally counted to ten and flopped into the chair. "So where am I supposed to see patients?"

"This is only a temporary setback—I've already made other arrangements."

"Oh . . . ?"

"Yes, temporary office space at the Digby, uh, Clinic."

"Wait a minute here." Taylor rubbed her forehead with thumb and forefinger. "You mean Digby already has a medical cli—"

"Well, not exactly. If you can meet me at 311 Drumond Avenue around noon, I'll explain everything. Because of the insurance, this is the only alternative."

*311 Drumond.* The address didn't sound familiar. Taylor weighed her options. *Zip. Zilch. Zero.* "Sure, Mr. Mayor."

"Everything's going to be just fine, Doctor."

Taylor mumbled something polite but noncommittal and hung up the phone. For some reason, she had the feeling Bradshaw was trying to pull one over on her.

"Paranoid." Shaking her head, she stood and grabbed her car keys. "Time to unpack." Then figure out how to get her medical bag back.

Painlessly.

Gordon hated being late. That alone would've been enough to ensure his foul mood, but running into Taylor this morning had really settled the matter.

His old Jeep had to go—that was all there was to it. This was the third morning in less than a month that he'd had to coast down the hill into town.

With Taylor's medical bag in tow, he climbed out of his Jeep and took a moment to peek through the front window to inventory his waiting room. Mrs. Johnson and her equally neurotic cat—just what he needed.

Drawing a deep breath, he mustered every shred of patience he could find, which didn't amount to much, and walked around to the rear entrance. The door swung open before he even found his key.

Not a good sign.

"Good morning."

Sue Wheeler's bubbly voice made him want to growl louder than his most cantankerous patient. "Good? Why are you always so . . . ?"

"Pleasant?" She grinned mischievously. "It's a tough job, but somebody's got to do it."

Sue was an excellent receptionist and a good friend, but sometimes her eternal cheerfulness was downright sickening. "I don't remember that being in your job description."

"When did you give me a job description? I have witnesses, you know." She held his lab coat out by the collar. "You said for me to answer that damn phone before it drove you insane. So I do, and I file charts and you pay me. Remember?"

Gordon dropped the medical bag on the corner table, then slipped into his lab coat. Max sniffed the medical bag and sighed. It wasn't food. The aging setter ambled off toward Gordon's office at the end of the hall, where he'd curl up on the rug and only move with the shift of the sun's rays.

*Lucky stiff.*

Gordon turned his attention back to Sue, an attractive single mother—they'd even dated a few times, but they remained just friends. She wanted romance and magic in a relationship, but, for whatever reasons, it hadn't happened between them. According to Sue, it wasn't in their stars.

*Stars. Magic. Bah humbug.* He'd had that once and a whole hell of a lot of good it had done him. In his opinion, romance and magic were highly overrated. What was wrong with . . . safe?

Of course, the events of ten years ago had created both a bond and a barrier between him and Sue.

And driven Taylor away.

He rubbed his chin, anchoring himself on the rasp of his beard against his fingers. *Get it straight, Lane.* Taylor's lack of trust had made her leave.

Too bad things hadn't worked out with Sue. He was crazy about her son. Ryan was without a doubt the most precocious ten-year-old in Digby since Gordon's eleventh birthday.

*Not in the stars.* But she'd been right—him liking her son wasn't sufficient grounds for a marriage. At least one of them had been sane enough to recognize that fact in time.

*Damn.*

He needed to work—anything to keep his mind off magic. And Taylor. "I saw Mrs. Johnson in the waiting room."

"Yeah. What a way to start the week." Sue shrugged and handed Gordon a stack of phone messages. "It's been slow for a Monday, but I'm sure things will pick up after lunch."

*Things have been pretty exciting already.* Gordon's gaze drifted to the medical bag and his gut twisted again. He couldn't get Taylor off his mind. All through college he'd thought of her, and after returning to Digby, he kept hoping. . . .

"Damn."

"So why are you late? Car trouble again?" Sue asked, clicking her tongue when he nodded. "When are you going to trade in that old thing?"

Gordon moved toward the door and looked back over his shoulder. "I guess it's time." He swallowed hard. "But it has . . . sentimental value."

"Huh. Don't I know it? You've been driving that Jeep since high school."

"Yeah." His voice sounded peculiar even to him. After clearing his throat, he added, "Time to put the past where it belongs, I suppose." *All of it.*

"Yeah, I suppose." She walked over to the corner table and lifted the medical bag.

His reference to the past had sent Sue into her cocoon. She had a way of pulling herself inward and he knew why. Hell, he envied her ability to shield herself from the hurt, though he suspected her protection was only superficial.

How would seeing Taylor again affect Sue?

"Nice bag. Is it new?" she asked.

*Changing the subject won't make the hurt go away.* "Yeah, but it isn't mine." Gordon clenched his teeth and drew a deep breath, holding it while Sue read the luggage tag.

"Dr. Bowen?" Sue gasped and dropped the tag, bringing her hand up to cover her mouth. "Oh, my—"

"She's the new doctor."

"Taylor?"

"Yes." Silence stretched between them as Gordon watched the fluctuating expressions in Sue's eyes.

"Well, that's good," she said, obviously trying to convince herself of that fact even more than him. "Women make the best doctors. Uh, doctors for *humans,* I mean." She tried to smile, but it was a poor imitation. "So you've already . . . seen her."

"Yeah." Gordon gnashed his teeth. Neither of them needed to rehash history right now—or ever, for that matter. It hurt too damned much. "I don't think I should keep Mrs. Johnson and Precious waiting any longer." Gordon opened the door and walked down the hall to the waiting room, knowing

Sue wasn't about to let the matter drop. Now that her memory was roused, her guilt would be as well.

Standing in the doorway that led to his waiting room, Gordon breathed a sigh of relief. Mrs. Johnson's Precious was still his only patient. Monday mornings were usually a three-ring circus, in direct contrast to the rest of the week, when more business would've been welcome. The truth was, Digby really didn't need a full-time veterinarian. It was all Gordon could do to pay the rent on the place.

"Good morning, Mrs. Johnson," he said, flashing her a smile. "I'm sorry I'm late this morning—car trouble."

Mrs. Johnson gathered her aging white cat in her arms and rose. She paused to give him the once-over. "Hmm. And I suppose it must take quite a while to put all that hair in a ponytail every morning, too." With her nose pointed in the air, Mrs. Johnson marched by.

"Yes, ma'am. It does take a few minutes." Gordon rolled his eyes heavenward. At least his day was consistent.

"Gordon, I'm glad I caught you," a loud male voice called above the bells jingling on the front door. "I need to talk to you. It's important."

"Wait your turn, Tom," Mrs. Johnson called over her shoulder. "Precious is having the vapors."

*Vapors?* Gordon met the mayor's gaze—the man's wide-eyed look of utter bewilderment was priceless. Mrs. Johnson must've been reading historical romances again. Month before last, she'd been convinced Precious was suffering from consumption.

"I'll be with you in a few minutes, Tom." Gordon patted the woman on the shoulder. "Precious needs me now."

"But she'll be here at noon," the mayor argued.

Gordon frowned and held the door open for Mrs. Johnson and her cat. He glanced at his watch and shook his head. "No, I don't think this will take that long."

Sue rolled her eyes and winked at Gordon on her way to the reception desk. "Mr. Mayor, what a pleasant surprise. Don't tell me your horse has colic again."

As the door closed behind him, Gordon thanked God for cheerful, diplomatic receptionists everywhere.

"Well"—he turned to face his patient and Mrs. Johnson—"tell me about Precious and her . . . vapors."

Taylor stood on the sidewalk and stared at the sign.

*Digby Veterinary Clinic.*

The mayor had left out one rather significant word when he told her where to meet him. After she double-checked the address, she paced in front of the building for a few minutes, glancing at her watch several times before squaring her shoulders to face the mayor.

This was too much. She couldn't practice medicine in an animal hospital.

Correction—she *wouldn't* practice medicine in an animal hospital. If the people of Digby truly wanted a doctor for humans, then they could make other arrangements. This was absurd.

Convinced she had her temper under control and her determination in place, Taylor pushed open the door and went inside. A string of small bells jingled to announce her arrival. Upon closer inspection, she realized it was a cat collar hooked to the door handle.

*Of course—what else?*

A large man rose from a chair near the receptionist's desk. His appearance matched the voice she'd heard on the phone earlier.

"Dr. Bowen?" he asked, extending his hand.

"Yes, and you must be Mayor Bradshaw." She held her voice carefully under control, then watched his huge paw swallow her hand in a vigorous handshake.

"I truly do apologize for this little inconvenience, but I'm sure we'll be able to arrange something here for a few weeks."

"Weeks?" Taylor echoed.

"Here?" the woman behind the desk repeated.

Taylor turned to face the receptionist. "Do you—" Her voice froze and a loud roar began in her ears. It couldn't be.

"Taylor."

"You two know each other?" the mayor asked.

Taylor looked at the floor and nodded. Why hadn't she considered the possibility of running into Gordon *and* Sue in Digby? It was a small town, after all.

Of course, she'd assumed they'd probably moved away, like most of her senior class. Digby didn't have a lot to offer in the way of a job market. This entire mess was too ironic for words.

"Yes, we . . . went to school together," Sue said, her voice quiet.

Taylor filled her lungs with air, then released it very slowly. If Sue could do this, so could she. Mustering her courage, she faced the woman again. "Do you know anything about this?"

Sue's mouth was set in a grim line and her eyes glittered. She looked as if she might burst into tears at any moment, but Taylor held her gaze and tried to make her own expression as impassive as possible.

"No," Sue finally said. "I don't have a clue, and I'm pretty sure G—my boss doesn't either."

Both women shifted their gazes back to the mayor. "Well?" they asked in unison.

The big man turned crimson and tugged at his collar. His bald head broke into a sweat and he pulled a handkerchief from his breast pocket to mop away the moisture.

With a shrug and a sheepish grin, the mayor faced Taylor. "I'm sorry, Dr. Bowen, but as I explained on the phone, the late snows and the insurance comp—"

"Yes, I understand that." Taylor drew a deep breath, searching her mind for another solution. "But you can't possibly expect human patients to be seen in a clinic intended for animals."

Taylor turned her attention, reluctantly, back to Sue. Being mature and professional was in direct conflict with the way she really wanted to behave right now. Still, the pained expression in Sue's eyes stayed her. Despite all the reasons Taylor should despise the woman, she couldn't bring herself to be deliberately cruel.

Sue shrugged. "We keep things quite sanitary here. We have lab, X ray, and even surgical facilities. I guess it sort of makes sense."

Taylor looked toward the ceiling. She couldn't believe her first experience away from the hospital where she'd done her residency would take place . . . in an animal hospital.

"I just don't see how we could keep things . . . separate." Taylor recognized and appreciated Sue's efforts to reach a viable solution to at least one mess. The other situation—the past—was irreparable. "The waiting room, for instance."

"This is a small town, Dr. Bowen," the mayor said, his voice quieter now. Subdued. "You know these people—folks are used to going places together. We only have one church, one grocery, one hardware store. . . ."

"One medical clinic for all species, with or without fur?" Taylor arched an eyebrow and held up her hands. "This is far from ideal, but why couldn't I see patients in my den temporarily?"

"Insurance." The mayor sighed, his expression forlorn. "I argued with Smith until I was blue in the face, but that son of a b—gun wouldn't budge. He's the one who thought of this place. Said it was simple to add you to this policy until the new clinic is done."

Taylor rolled her eyes heavenward. She'd been warned about insurance companies and doctors. "So I have no choice." *Now there's determination.*

"So it would seem," Sue said, tapping her pencil

against her knuckles. Her face was almost as red as her hair. "But the mayor hasn't mentioned this to my boss yet. Remember him? You know, the guy who pays the rent, the equipment, signs my paycheck . . . ?"

"Well, I'm sure once I explain the situation, he'll understand," the mayor offered, rocking back on his heels with a smug expression on his face.

*The old coot told me he'd already made other arrangements.*

Sue stood and moved to the back of the room. Turning to look directly at Taylor, she said, "Wait here—I just remembered something."

*Yeah, I'll bet.* For once in her life, Taylor wished she had a bad memory—or at least a selective one. The receptionist disappeared through the doorway, then emerged a moment later with Taylor's leather medical bag.

"How did you get my—"

Another door opened at the opposite end of the tiled waiting room and a small gray-haired woman emerged with a white cat cradled in her arms. "Oh, but Precious hates cat food, Doctor."

"Yes, I can tell from her weight," a man said from behind the woman.

The male voice washed over Taylor and she suddenly felt cold all over. *Oh, my God.*

"Now, I want you to promise me you'll keep Precious on this new diet, Mrs. Johnson."

"She'll starve."

"There's no way this cat will starve herself, but she

might very well eat herself into an early grave. Trust me, she'll eat this when she gets hungry enough."

The woman and her cat stepped to the side and a tall man wearing a white coat walked out behind them.

"Gordon," Taylor whispered. She rubbed her forehead, wondering how she managed to end up in these situations. He was a veterinarian. She should've known. It was what he'd always wanted. . . .

In a town the size of Digby, running into people she knew was unavoidable. Still, this had passed uncomfortable and was moving at warp speed toward a major violation of cruel and unusual punishment.

She shot Sue an accusing glare, but the woman's trembling chin and silent tears curbed Taylor's harsh words. Why hadn't Sue told her?

"Not even a little tuna?" the woman pleaded.

"Not even that."

"Poor Precious."

"Will be much healthier on this diet. Try it for a month; then we'll see how she's doing and discuss it again. Okay?"

"Oh, all right."

Gordon walked Mrs. Johnson to the door, then turned toward the reception desk. "All right, Tom," he said, taking a few steps before he froze to stare. His gaze traveled from Taylor to the mayor to Sue, then back to Taylor again. "Taylor?"

"Gordon."

"You two know each other, too?" the mayor asked, sounding disgustingly pleased with this turn of events.

"Yes," they said simultaneously.

"Well, this oughta make things a lot easier on all of us then." Bradshaw walked over to slap the vet on the back. "See, Gordon, the new clinic won't be finished for a few weeks, so we were—"

"We?" Taylor asked, wanting to make certain Gordon knew she'd played no part in this torturous plan.

The mayor shot her an apologetic look. "All right, *I* wondered if you'd mind sharing your clinic with Dr. Bowen until then, because Smith won't cover her anywhere else."

"Share . . . my clinic?" Gordon's eyes grew round and his face darkened. "With . . ."

"Dr. Bowen." The mayor chuckled and shook his head. "My secretary told me this is a homecoming for the doc. I should've realized she'd have friends here already. Now isn't this going to work out great?"

Gordon's gaze shifted from the mayor to Taylor again. He looked trapped. Angry.

Desperate.

*I don't believe this.*

But they were adults now—all his lies, his false promises, and his betrayal had taken place over ten years ago. She was mature enough to handle this. Besides, what choice did she have? If they were going to work together, they had to at least be civil to each other.

"She says she's only staying for the term of the contract, but I'm hoping we can change her mind." Bradshaw chuckled and winked, oblivious to the tension in the air.

"I see." Gordon folded his arms in front of him and looked away, making Taylor squirm inwardly.

Undaunted, the mayor continued, "Dr. Bowen here was a little worried about this being clean enough, but—"

"*Clean* enough?" Gordon snapped his head around to stare at her.

"Uh-oh." Sue ducked her auburn head, reached for a stack of files, and started to sort them.

"Well, I didn't exactly *say* that," Taylor began, realizing too late that this was a sensitive issue.

"When was the last time you visited a real doctor's office, *Doctor?*" He took another step—so close she could smell the faint hint of soap on his skin. Soap . . . and something else. Something more intimate.

Gordon himself.

"How long, Taylor?" he repeated.

"Years." She sighed and shook her head. All her medical experience had taken place in a hospital environment. Until now.

"I doubt most of them have operating rooms. *Sterile* operating rooms."

Taylor blinked but resisted the impulse to take a backward step. She hated to admit it, but he was absolutely right. "I apologize, *Dr.* Lane," she said slowly, lifting the corners of her mouth in a smug smile, knowing what she had to do. "You're right and I stand corrected."

"I am? You do?"

Gordon's surprise at her admission left him momentarily vulnerable. For some reason—pride?—she couldn't resist the sudden need to demonstrate to him and Sue that she was completely over her broken heart. She was beyond all that now.

"Yes, you're absolutely right. For routine medical care, I'm sure this facility will be more than adequate. Where shall I hang my stethoscope?" *God, give me strength. Fast.*

Gordon arched a brow and his expression of astonishment shifted to one of mild amusement. His mouth twitched suggestively. "Follow me, Doctor." Beyond the slight twitching, his lips barely moved until he flashed her a cat-that-ate-the-canary grin.

*Taylor, you're in big trouble.*

# THREE

They were alone.

This wasn't at all what Taylor'd had in mind when she agreed to follow Gordon down the hall and into the back of his clinic.

Gordon pushed open a door and familiar, sterile scents greeted Taylor. "This is the operating room. Satisfactory, Doctor?"

"Gordon, I'm sorry. I . . . I made an assumption." She looked inside the immaculate room. "Obviously, an erroneous one." She touched his upper arm and immediately regretted it. His warmth radiated into her hand, making her yearn to maintain the connection.

He lowered his gaze to her hand on his arm. She saw his Adam's apple bob up and down in his throat—a gleam of perspiration coated his forehead.

When he looked at her again, his expression was different. The indignation that had driven him a few moments earlier was now curiously absent, replaced by something that snatched all the air from her lungs. The passion she'd seen in his eyes this morning had returned.

With a vengeance.

This morning, it might have been the circumstances more than anything that made him look at her like a man who wanted something above and beyond simple conversation. Now it was more.

Much more.

She swallowed the lump in her throat and licked her parched lips. So many shared experiences.

So much pain.

The intensity in his eyes suddenly faded. He blinked and looked at her again. "Well? Do the facilities meet with your approval?"

His tone and his words reminded Taylor that this was *his* clinic and she was the intruder. "It's very professional. Besides, barring a major emergency, I'm not planning to perform surgery." She allowed her arm to fall to her side, leaving her strangely bereft.

He closed the door and walked farther down the hall. "This is the kennel." His tone was all business now. "I don't imagine you'll have much need for this part of the clinic."

"No, probably not." Taylor's eyes burned, but she focused on her surroundings, banishing thoughts of what had been. And what could have been. Why was she doing this to herself?

"Hey there, fella." He stopped at a large pen. "How are you doing today, Patches?"

Forcing her misery into submission, Taylor turned her attention to the beautiful spaniel in the pen. "He's gorgeous."

"Yeah, I think so."

"Is he yours?"

Gordon sighed and reached in to scratch the dog behind the ears. "No, Max wouldn't put up with that." Patches looked at Gordon with eyes of adoration.

Taylor could relate.

"He's mine."

Taylor's heart vaulted into her throat as she whirled around to confront the newcomer. A boy—preteen, she guessed—stood in the doorway staring at them with an insolent expression.

"Ryan, why aren't you in school?" Gordon straightened, ignoring the dog's whimper for continued attention.

"It's lunch. I came to see Patches." The boy's voice cracked, eliciting a surge of compassion from Taylor, though she had no idea why. "Is he gonna be all right?"

Gordon looked down for a moment, then faced Ryan. "He's doing better, but I'll know more when the tests come back from UNC. Does your mom know you're here?"

*Mom?* Taylor watched Gordon for a clue. A terrible suspicion slithered through her, making her want to run away. Sue's son?

"Well . . ." The boy lowered his eyes and shuffled his feet. "Nope."

"So Sue doesn't know you're playing hooky?"

"I'll get back before she sees me."

*Sue and Gordon's son?*

"Too late. I saw you." Sue's head appeared over the boy's and she ruffled his curly red hair. "Only for a minute, Ryan. You're going to be late getting back to school. English, right?"

"Yeah." Ryan grumbled and shifted his feet, then looked up at Gordon.

"Go ahead." Gordon smiled and inclined his head toward the dog. "This mutt's begging for attention. Give him some."

"Cool!"

Taylor stepped back as Ryan made a beeline for the pen and threw open the door. The boy's entire face lit up with love. Patches wagged his tail and jumped up and down, whimpering.

She caught sight of the look on Gordon's face and wondered again about his relationship to the boy. And to Sue. There was no physical resemblance to Gordon, but the child looked about the right age.

Her stomach burned and her cheeks felt hot. She was over that chapter in her life, and it was high time she took control of her emotions. *Now, Taylor.*

They all followed Ryan to Gordon's office. "So when can I take him home?" Ryan asked.

"I see no reason why you can't take him home today after school."

"All *right!*" Ryan absolutely beamed at Gordon and flashed his mother a broad smile. "Did you hear that, Mom?"

"Yes, I heard." Sue's expression as she looked over her son's head was solemn. "You'd better wash your hands and get back to school."

"I know." Ryan rolled his eyes. "I'll be back after school to pick up Patches."

Ryan paused to look at Taylor, as if just now seeing her for the first time. "Who's she?"

"Well, how rude." Sue shook her head and looked down, avoiding Taylor's questioning glance.

Taylor stepped forward to extend her hand to the boy. "I'm Taylor Bowen." *Are you Gordon's child?*

The boy shook her hand, then walked to the corner sink to wash. Sue handed him a paper towel as he turned around.

"Taylor used to live here," Sue explained with only a slight catch in her voice. "She's the new doctor."

Ryan's eyes grew huge and his mouth fell open. The red hair and freckles gave him an impish, *Little Rascals* quality. "A *girl?*"

Gordon, Sue, and Taylor all laughed, albeit somewhat nervously, but Ryan stood his ground. "I ain't taking my clothes off when I go to the doctor. No, sirree."

"Don't say 'ain't.' " Sue tousled his hair again.

Taylor summoned a serious expression, not difficult when she remembered Ryan's possible paternity. "I assure you, Ryan, that I won't ask you to remove all your clothes unless it's a matter of life and death."

Taylor met Gordon's eyes. Big mistake. His gaze locked with hers, transporting her back in time again. They'd been so young. So much in love.

So . . . passionate.

Heat crept up her neck to her ears and she snatched herself from Gordon's spell. When she glanced back at Ryan, she saw suspicion written clearly on his face. The boy looked from Taylor to Gordon, then back to Taylor.

"You coming over for dinner this evening?" Ryan asked Gordon.

"I, uh, wasn't invited." Gordon flashed Sue a grin.

*They aren't married.* An irrational surge of relief eddied through Taylor. Divorced? There was no way the Gordon she knew would stand by and not claim his own child. Not a chance. She searched Sue's eyes for possible answers to her questions.

Sue's blush deepened and she drew a deep breath. Even from across the room, Taylor knew the woman was trembling. She met Taylor's gaze, her eyes wide and almost pleading.

Taylor blinked and looked again. Was Sue afraid Taylor would tell Ryan what had happened ten years ago? Though she had every reason to be upset—and she had been—she wasn't a vindictive person. Surely Sue remembered that about Taylor. She gave a slight shake of her head, hoping to dispel the woman's concern. The last thing in the world Taylor wanted was to shatter a young boy's image of his own mother.

No matter who she was . . . or what she'd done.

Sue gave Taylor an unsteady smile. "I think you should *both* come to dinner."

Gordon shifted uneasily, and Taylor's blush went from hot to molten. Searching for an excuse, she said, "Oh, I really couldn't—"

"Nonsense." Sue took her son's arm and started out the door. "We have to get it through this kid's head that women are every bit as smart as men."

"Ah, Mom."

Sue paused to look over her shoulder, ignoring her son's protests. The look she flashed Taylor was filled with gratitude . . . and something more. Regret?

"Have her there at six, Gordon. I have work to do, and this young man has to get back to school. I think lunch is over. Hmm?"

The door closed, leaving Taylor and Gordon alone again.

Gordon glanced sideways at her. "Sue's . . ."

"Trying too hard?" Taylor finished, leaning against the edge of his desk, determined to maintain her composure. She'd be gracious and sophisticated about all this.

No matter what.

"Looks like we're stuck with each other this evening," she finally said, hating the way her voice sounded.

Something flared in his eyes, fleeting but powerful.

"I'm really sorry for getting you into this," she said when he remained silent. *Why am I apologizing to him?* She was the one who'd been betrayed all those years ago.

Gordon walked around his desk and opened a drawer. "Nothing for you to be sorry about." After a few seconds of shuffling around, he pulled out a key and passed it to her, his fingers brushing against hers with a jolt. "Fits the front and back doors."

"Thanks." Taylor closed her hand around the key. "This must be . . . uncomfortable for you."

He met her gaze and held it—possessed it, really. "Taylor, I . . ." Sighing, he shrugged and looked away. "I suppose it's fate."

*Fate.* She didn't know exactly what he meant by that, but for some inane reason her breath quickened and liquid warmth settled low in her middle. This stuff wasn't meant for her—for them. Not anymore.

"Fate?" she echoed, hating the throaty tone her voice had suddenly acquired. "This morning by the stream, my medical bag, the clinic, and now you have to take me to dinner at Sue's house? That's way above and beyond the call of duty, even for fate."

Gordon chuckled and his expression warmed. "This would probably make a good movie."

"Yeah, black comedy."

They both laughed, and Taylor welcomed the respite from the tension. It was good to hear his laughter, even though more unanswered questions continued to plague her. One in particular.

Hiding her sense of loss, she stood and turned toward the door. "Well, I'd better find a place to unpack my supplies." She smiled, hoping he didn't see through her facade. "Can you point me to an examining room I might borrow for a while?"

Gordon looked nervous as he stood and followed her into the hall. "Actually, there are two connecting rooms at the end of the hall we hardly ever use."

"Perfect—an office and an examining room." Taylor let him lead, admiring his long, jeans-clad legs and beautiful hair. "Since this is only temporary, there won't be time to have a second phone line run, or for me to hire someone to answer it, so I want to pay Sue something for the extra work."

"That sounds fair."

*So far, so good.* "And I'll . . . try not to bother you any more than absolutely necessary."

Gordon stopped suddenly and turned to her. "Taylor, that isn't possible . . . and you know it."

He brought his hands to the level of her shoulders and froze. A deluge of conflicting emotions showed plainly in his eyes. It both frightened and delighted her at the same time.

His probing scrutiny searched, bore into her and tugged at feelings she'd wanted so desperately to keep buried. Safe. Unscathed.

"I'll still try," she said quietly, severing the invisible thread that had momentarily connected them.

Visibly shaking himself, he dropped his hands and opened the nearest door. "You can use this as an office—there's no desk, but there's a table and chair."

"And a window. Thanks. It'll be fine." She rubbed the back of her neck and stretched, closing her eyes. "That long drive is catching up with me."

"You probably want to rest before this evening."

"Good idea." Was she really going to Sue's house for dinner—*with* Gordon? *Be tough, Taylor.* She forced a smile, then peeked into the adjoining room. "Ah, good. Cabinets for my supplies."

"Are they in your car? I'll help you bring them in now; then I have to get ready for my afternoon patients . . . if there are any."

"Thanks." Taylor edged past him, unable to avoid brushing against his arm. The urge to turn toward him and snuggle close nearly overtook her. Gordon had always been so cuddly and affectionate.

Squelching her raging hormones and volatile emotions, she walked down the hall and through the waiting room. Digging her car keys from the pocket of her jeans, she hurried to her Volkswagen. Infuriatingly, her hands trembled, making her drop the keys in the dirt near her feet.

"Here, I'll get them." Gordon bent to retrieve her keys.

*Always the gentleman.* Like a knife, the pain renewed itself, but she was determined to bury it deep so he wouldn't see. As he straightened, their eyes met and held; then he flashed her a weak smile that destroyed the moment.

"Let's get your stuff," he said.

She popped the trunk and watched Gordon remove her box of medical supplies. The muscles in his arms rippled through the white fabric of his lab coat.

Time had definitely been kind to Gordon Lane.

"Where should I pick you up this evening?" he asked, holding the heavy box. "You didn't say."

Flashing him a mischievous grin, she tried to ignore the pain-riddled thunder of her heart. "Same place you did last time."

Gordon brought his Jeep to a stop in front of the small Victorian house and stared. Talk about déjà vu.

Same house. Same Jeep. Same girl . . .

No, not a girl—a woman now. Very much so. Taylor the girl had haunted him all his adult life. Now the woman she'd become was turning his simple, well-ordered life into an adults-only version of *Alice in Wonderland.*

And he'd definitely followed that white rabbit.

Remembering warm summer nights long past, he allowed himself a more leisurely stroll down Memory Lane. A stroll where hormones ran amok, and young bodies explored each other in every sense of the word. . . .

Gordon's blood supply redirected itself, pooling and throbbing until he had to shift uncomfortably to accommodate his responsive body. Angry with his inability to control his emotions or his physical reaction—just like a teenager—he climbed out of the Jeep and leaned against it.

"History's history," he muttered. No matter how sweet or painful the memories, they couldn't change the fact that Taylor hadn't trusted him. Besides, the future she'd chosen for herself didn't include him or Digby.

Tom Bradshaw's words returned to torment Gordon. *"She says she's only staying for the term of the contract, but I'm hoping we can change her mind."*

Scowling at himself and at the past, Gordon stepped onto the sidewalk and opened the gate. The scent of roses touched his nostrils, and he remembered Taylor's dress for their senior prom. Her mother had made it, and Gordon thought it the most beautiful one he'd ever seen, not that he had ever been much of an authority on women's clothing. Of course, now he realized the beauty he'd seen had been in the wearer, not the dress.

She'd worn tiny rosebuds in her hair. He drew another deep breath and closed his eyes against the continuing battle between past and present.

"Enough."

Shoving one hand into his pocket, he marched up the walk and rapped on the door. He was finished dwelling on the past. Taylor was home now, but not for long.

The door opened and he tried to smile. Taylor stood staring at him through the screen, an expression of uncertainty making her look so much like the girl he'd last seen framed in this doorway.

"Good evening," he said, wishing the sun had already set. Darkness might help hide his turmoil and the pang of recollection.

"Evening," she returned, pushing open the screen. "Come in for a second while I grab my sweater."

Reluctantly, Gordon followed her into the all-too-familiar living room; then she rushed up the stairs, leaving him alone again with the past. His throat felt full and his stomach gave a decisive lurch. *Damn.*

Looking around the room, he found the piano and was once again transported into the past.

"I'm ready."

Then he saw her standing at the bottom of the stairs. Dressed in a print skirt and green knit top, with a white sweater slung over her arm, she looked . . .

Incredible.

He swallowed hard and tried to deny himself the

pleasure of allowing his hungry gaze to linger on the shape of her breasts beneath the clinging fabric. His impudent and infuriating memory provided his imagination with her hidden attributes.

In minute detail.

"I hope this is all right," she said quietly, prompting Gordon to look up at her lovely face.

"Uh, you look fine." The truth was, she looked a whole hell of a lot better than fine, but that was dangerous territory. "Sue's strictly the casual type."

"Yeah, I sort of remembered that."

She smiled in a sad way that tugged at something he knew was better off left buried deep in his subconscious. Unfortunately, today he seemed to have very little control over anything his mind decided to summon.

Maybe once the initial shock of having her home again wore off, he'd be able to control his thoughts a little better. Sure, that made sense. Drawing a deep breath, he squared his shoulders and smiled. "It's only across town, but we don't want to be late if we know what's good for us."

Crimson crept up her neck to her cheeks, and Gordon couldn't help but wonder what he'd said to cause her to blush. Or maybe she'd noticed the direction of his gaze a few minutes ago. With superhuman effort, he resisted the urge to look again.

They stepped outside and he pulled the door to, then she inserted the key and sent the dead bolt home. Such extreme security measures seemed out of place in Digby, but whoever owned the house now obviously didn't agree.

"Oh, I don't believe this." Taylor stood on the porch and stared at his Jeep. "The same one?"

The expression of utter delight on her face would be his undoing. He was as good as nuked.

"Yep, same one." He followed her down the walk and through the gate. Without hesitation, she climbed into the passenger side, her smile triggering more memories.

Another dangerous thought struck him as he walked around the front of the Jeep and climbed into the driver's seat. Besides his mom, Taylor was the only living person in the world who shared his love for this old Jeep. She'd shared his love *in* this old Jeep. The memory was as vivid as it had been that summer.

"I can't believe it's the same one." Her laughter crawled right into him, igniting feelings of warmth and affection, contrary to his emotional Armageddon.

*I'm in big trouble.*

"Buckle up," he said, struggling against the urge to gather her into his arms. After fastening his own seat belt and hearing the reassuring click of hers, he started the engine and dropped the Jeep into gear.

He ventured a side glance at her before pulling away from the curb. Dammit, she was still smiling. Why couldn't she be rude and arrogant? Or ugly? That would've been even better. Safer.

But no. She was drop-dead gorgeous, with the same wholesome beauty she'd always had, plus the added enhancement of full-blown womanhood.

His groin tightened again and he knew with the

utmost certainty that he could now pronounce himself fully recovered from this morning's ant attack. All systems go.

*For a one-way mission to nowhere.*

Silently cursing his own weaknesses, Gordon drove the few short blocks to Sue's house. On the edge of town nearest his cabin, the modest brick ranch sat back off the road in a pine grove.

"Here we are." He pulled into the drive and parked next to a strange car. Looking again as he cut the engine, Gordon groaned. Correction, the midsize sedan wasn't strange at all.

It was painfully familiar.

"What's wrong?" Taylor asked, reaching out to touch the back of his wrist with cool fingers. "You feel all right?"

"No, I don't think either of us is going to feel all right after we go inside." He turned to Taylor with a sigh. "Guess who's coming to dinner?" The setting sun bathed her in shadow, but he still saw her bewildered frown.

"Well, I guess we are," she said.

Gordon jabbed his thumb over his shoulder at the blue sedan. "Unless someone else Sue knows has the very same car, which I doubt in a town the size of this one, we're about to . . ."

"To *what?*" She wrapped her fingers around his wrist and squeezed hard. "Gordon Lane, stop teasing me and tell me whose car that is."

He rolled his eyes heavenward, then looked at her. "My mother's."

"Oh." Taylor fell back against her seat, releasing him at the same time. "That means . . ."

"Yep." Gordon gripped the steering wheel with both hands. "That means she's heard about you being here, and I'll bet Ryan's gotten an earful, too."

"About . . . us," she said unnecessarily. Her sigh equaled his own. "This should be interesting."

"I'd say that's an understatement-and-a-half." He started to chuckle; then the more he thought about it, the louder he laughed.

"What's so funny?"

He turned to look at her shocked expression. "All of this."

"All of what?"

"This. Us. The *irony.*" Gordon's laughter died in his throat. "Think about it, Taylor." His voice fell to a whisper. "Think about it."

His blood roared through his veins, screaming, "Kiss her, kiss her, kiss her." He'd like nothing better. All sense of reason fled, and he reached out to touch her cheek with the backs of his fingers. So soft . . .

*But she left me—didn't trust me.*

Still, he couldn't stop himself from touching her, savoring the feel of her skin. Recollections and pain bombarded him until he could barely breathe.

Taylor leaned into his caress, and he brought his other hand to her opposite cheek. This felt so right, almost as if she'd never left.

But she had left.

No, he wouldn't listen to that vindictive voice. Not now. At this moment, all he wanted was to taste her lips, to see if she was as sweet now as before.

"Gordon?"

The sound of her voice fueled his need and he inched toward her. Closer. Closer. Closer.

*Bam!*

A loud thump on the Jeep's hood made them both leap back, gasping. The sun was low enough now to trigger the motion detector on the floodlight. Gordon squinted at the harsh interruption.

"Hey, Gordon." Ryan slapped the hood of the Jeep again. "Hurry and come inside. Your mom's here. Boy, she sure knows a lot of stories. 'Course, I don't believe half of 'em."

"Hmm. Yeah, I'm sure she does." Gordon looked over at Taylor and saw the rapid rise and fall of her chest, though she kept her face averted. They'd come so close.

So close to making a big mistake.

*Damn.* He didn't need this. His blood pressure undoubtedly hit the critical point as he wondered how he'd ever survive this evening with the woman who'd broken his heart ten years ago, the woman who wasn't interested in him as anything more than a friend, and his mother.

All in one place at the same time.

# FOUR

Taylor held her breath as she followed Gordon to the aqua front door. He'd almost kissed her, and she would have let him. What had come over her? High school madness? She was an adult now. She could handle this.

*Get tough, Taylor.*

Sue gave her a nervous smile, and Taylor remembered to breathe just in time to prevent a blackout. She had to face the past, the present, the future.

*And Gordon's mother.*

"Thank you for inviting me," she said, though her thoughts were just the opposite. Why had she let Sue talk her into this? Oh, hell, she knew why. Because she had to live among these people for the next three years, and making peace—or at least proving she could ignore the past—was a prerequisite to continued sanity. Hers.

"Hi, Taylor." Sue's voice sounded subdued, but her smile was open and genuine. "I'm glad you could come. Priscilla is here. She's in the kitchen."

"Yeah, we heard," Gordon said from behind Taylor.

Ryan bounded past with a toy airplane, making

noises Taylor hadn't realized a human could produce. Of course, her mother'd often said that little boys could sometimes be called humanesque. Now Taylor understood why. Her own brother had been two years older, but she did remember more than a few incidences of somewhat inhuman behavior.

A smile of remembrance tugged at her lips and she looked around Sue's tidy living room. The beige-and-mauve decor was warm and homey. One wall boasted photos of Ryan at various ages, from infancy to present. A cast-iron wood stove occupied one corner. Summer evenings at this altitude often included a warm fire.

"Dinner's almost ready," Sue said, turning toward the kitchen. "I thought we'd eat on the back porch, since it's so nice this evening."

"Something smells great," Gordon said, taking Taylor's elbow and steering her toward the kitchen. "If I ate here every night, I'd weigh three hundred pounds."

*Why don't you eat here every night?* Taylor cast him a sidelong glance and swallowed the lump of trepidation lodged in her throat. Unanswered questions tormented her.

The kitchen was clean and spacious, with white cabinets, appliances, and ceramic tile. A blue stenciled design adorned the woodwork, giving the room a country French appearance. Of course, Sue had always been artistic.

Taylor tried to nudge aside reflections of their teen years, when she and Sue had been practically inseparable. In some ways, losing her best friend had hurt almost as much as losing her first love. She drew a sharp breath and released it slowly.

"Sue, shall I dress the salad?" Priscilla Lane asked as she stepped through the back door.

"No, we'll let everybody do their own." Sue took a tray and slipped behind Priscilla and out the back door.

Priscilla's lips pressed into a thin line as her son bent and kissed her on the cheek.

"Hi, Mom. Surprised to see you here."

Mrs. Lane patted Gordon's shoulder and inclined her head—an impossibly tight array of frosty curls—toward Taylor. "So you came home at last, I see."

"It's good to see you again, Mrs. Lane." Taylor's pulse thrummed in her ears and perspiration coated the back of her neck. Once upon a time, Priscilla Lane had been like a second mother to her. "I'm here temporarily."

"Three years, I hear." Mrs. Lane lifted her bony shoulders in a shrug. "Think you can manage that long, or will you run away again?"

"Mom." Gordon's voice held a warning, but it went unheeded.

"It's the truth." Mrs. Lane lifted her chin, her bright blue eyes piercing Taylor. "She ran away once—she could do it again." She tilted her head to one side and arched a silver brow. "Just don't take my boy's heart with you this time."

"Maybe I should just—"

"Cowards always run," the older woman said, pivoting to grab the salad dressing and a stack of blue gingham napkins. "You come from good stock.

Show us some of your family's backbone, Dr. Bowen. Show us the girl you used to be."

Without another word, Mrs. Lane vanished through the back door again. Gordon met Taylor's gaze, his expression part apologetic and part something she couldn't define.

*Mrs. Lane is right, and I'm no coward.* She squared her shoulders and drew a shaky breath. If she didn't let Gordon and Sue matter, they couldn't hurt her again.

But they did matter. Both of them.

Ryan zoomed through again, still playing with his airplane. "Patches is sure glad to be home," the boy said as his plane took a nosedive, then shot straight up with appropriate sound effects.

"Is he out back?" Gordon turned his attention to the child.

"Yep, but he gets to sleep in my bed tonight." Ryan grinned. "Mom said he could, since he's been sick."

Gordon chuckled and patted Ryan's shoulder. The child stopped moving at last. "Remind me to have a look at him before I leave."

"Sure." Ryan resumed his trip to Mars through the back door. "I'm starved."

"Let's eat," Gordon said.

He gave Taylor a lingering look that drifted down the front of her sweater and made her face—and other regions—flame. She realized his mind wasn't on food, and the thoughts ricocheting through her brain and libido definitely didn't require salad dressing. Well . . .

"Dinner?" He pointed toward the back door. "They're waiting for us."

She shook herself and licked her suddenly dry lips. *Yep, I've gone way too long without a man.* Combing her fingers through her hair, she strode past Gordon and onto the screened-in porch. Lamps burned at both ends of the enclosure, and a long table was set with white pottery and blue gingham.

"You sit there, Taylor." Sue pointed to a chair at the far end of the table. "Gordon?" She indicated the chair on the corner beside Taylor. Ryan and his plane made a low pass. "Park it right there, flyboy."

The child obediently dropped into a chair between his mother and Priscilla Lane. Apparently food was not only the key to a man's heart, but also an effective means of controlling wayward boys. Taylor made a mental note.

Gordon's long legs brushed against hers as he took his seat. He shifted his knee away from hers, but his heat radiated through space and zeroed in on her without benefit of physical contact.

Why? He wasn't making a pass, touching her, trying to touch her, or showing any indication that he wanted to touch her. Why did she react so to his nearness?

Past experience? Of course, what else could it be? Taylor squared her shoulders, plucked her napkin from the table, and placed it in her lap. Resolutely, she looked around the table until her gaze rested on Gordon's mother.

Taylor Bowen was no coward.

Tonight was for appearances only. After this, she

would avoid social engagements involving the past. She had to. She peeked at Gordon through veiled lashes. He was staring at her again, and the pressure in her chest grew.

Yes, if she avoided these situations, she might actually survive this assignment. It would be easier to avoid personal entanglements at the clinic, and that was only temporary. Soon she would be at the new clinic and wouldn't have to see Gordon, Sue, Ryan, or Mrs. Lane at all, except as possible patients. She'd be all right until then, though the thought of playing doctor with Gordon raised her temperature a few degrees.

*"Playing" doctor is not allowed, Taylor.*

Beneath the table, Gordon clenched his napkin into a tight wad as he struggled with the onslaught of emotions. How much of this crap could a man take in one day? And his day had started damned early with Taylor's surprise visit this morning.

"Sue tells me that fool Tom Bradshaw wants Taylor to practice at your clinic," his mother said, forking salad onto her plate.

"That's right." Gordon took a roll from the basket in front of him and passed it.

"How long will this office sharing go on?" The expression in his mother's eyes was accusing.

*Like I asked for this?* "Until the clinic is completed." He glanced at Taylor, immediately wishing he could shut his mother up. Mom's questions were tormenting them both.

"The mayor didn't say, exactly," Taylor said, passing the butter dish to Gordon. "I forgot to ask, but I'll do that tomorrow."

His mother took the butter dish from Gordon and rolled her eyes. "Well, tending people in an animal hospital is mighty ridiculous, if you ask me."

*Which we didn't.* Gordon took a bite of his roll and it stuck in his craw. He quickly washed it down with iced tea, wondering how he'd managed to end up seated beside Taylor. Suspicion niggled through him and he shot a glance in Sue's direction. *Uh-oh.*

Was she? Could she? *Would* she?

Sue's cheeks turned crimson beneath his scrutiny. Dear God, the woman really was trying to play matchmaker. He sighed and shook his head, hoping she would catch on, but she jumped to her feet.

"I'll get the lasagna. Spinach. I hope that's all right with everybody."

"Sounds lovely." Taylor shifted in her chair and her knee brushed against his. She jerked back as if burned.

Gordon would deal with Sue later. Realizing that Taylor was as uncomfortable as he was disturbed him. He inched his legs closer to his mother, hoping to spare Taylor further distress.

Hell, why *should* he spare her? She was the one who up and left ten years ago. She was the one who made the choice to abandon him and everything they'd meant to each other. No, let her squirm. The more, the better, in fact.

He maneuvered his legs back directly in front of him.

She slid hers away.

He stretched his right leg out, his calf finding her shin. There, that was better. He forked salad into his mouth and chewed on a cherry tomato, casting her a surreptitious glance from the corner of his eye. Her face was as red as the tomato.

*Suffer.* A small voice in the back of his mind told him that he was being rude, and even unreasonable, but he told it to shut up and let him have his revenge. After all those years of hoping she would come back to him . . .

Yes, revenge was sweet. He rubbed his calf against her shin very slightly so it could pass as an accident. *Oh, yeah.* Revenge could be very sweet indeed, as long as it didn't backfire.

"Taylor, how are your folks? I've missed your mother, though she sends a Christmas letter every year."

His mother's voice made Gordon flinch inwardly, as if he was Ryan's age again and she'd caught him with his hand in the cookie jar. Of course, Taylor Bowen had become his cookie of choice around age sixteen. He focused on her again, noting the glisten of moisture along the side of her neck. He twitched his lips, wanting to taste her. *Damn.*

"They're fine, Mrs. Lane."

"Call me Priscilla, please. You used to. And how about that handsome brother of yours? Mike, isn't it?"

"He's practicing medicine in Denver, actually."

"Denver?" His mother looked appalled—not unusual. "And he hasn't come for a visit? That's only fifty miles from here."

"He's very busy, but he'll come up to visit me, I'm sure." She smiled. "In fact, he's promised to help me secure a research grant. Uh, if I don't go back east, that is."

"But what about Digby?"

Taylor blinked and played with her napkin. "I'm only here for three years. Remember?"

"Well, perhaps you'll change your mind before then," his mother said. "About a lot of things."

*What the devil . . . ?* His mother's voice sounded much calmer and friendlier now. She was treating Taylor as if nothing had ever happened. In fact, it seemed as if she suddenly wanted them to—

*No.*

"I'm sorry I was hard on you earlier, but it's a mother's instinct to protect her young."

Gordon coughed and grabbed his iced tea again.

"And though Gordon is pushing thirty—"

"Twenty-nine," he corrected, then chomped on a piece of ice with all his suppressed fury.

"Like I said, pushing thirty," his mother continued unruffled, "he'll always be my little boy."

Ryan let out a hoot and a snort.

"Watch it, squirt," Gordon growled. "Thanks, Mom, but in case you haven't noticed, I'm big enough to take care of myself now."

"So *you* say."

Gordon placed his face in his hands and groaned. "I don't believe this."

"You aren't the only one."

Taylor's voice surprised him, and he looked between his fingers. Her face was still flushed, her eyes snapped, and her lips were pressed into a thin line.

She was pissed, just like that time her brother had borrowed her bike without asking, then left it at the curb, where the trash truck ran over it.

"Mrs. Lane—Priscilla—I think there's a lot more to what happened ten years ago than you realize." Taylor drew a breath and placed her hands palms down on the table. "I definitely didn't return to harm your . . . *little boy.*"

Taylor's gaze shifted to him on the last two words. Gordon groaned again. Ryan laughed louder than before.

Mom stiffened, then gave a grudging nod. "All right, Taylor. Welcome home, then."

"What's going on?" Sue asked.

Gordon uncovered his face and watched their hostess place a steaming casserole dish on the table. "You don't want to know."

Sue glanced from Taylor to Gordon's mother. "Yep, you got that right." She picked up the serving spoon. "Who wants lasagna?"

Gordon sighed and looked at Taylor again. She chewed her salad furiously, her eyes dancing with victory. He held his breath as she slipped her foot out of her sandal and rubbed it along his leg.

She was playing dirty, and his body responded with infuriating enthusiasm.

"Lasagna, Gordon?" Sue asked.

He gave her a weak smile. "Got any crow?"

\* \* \*

After consuming two glasses of wine and reliving every school play and significant event from kindergarten through high school with Priscilla—the woman definitely seemed to have recovered from her unreasonable anger—Taylor was ready to call it a night. Besides, tomorrow was her first day as a real, practicing physician.

Even if it would be in an animal hospital.

However, she was quite pleased with the way tensions had eased as the evening progressed. No blood drawn by either side, even during the cleanup with three women in the kitchen.

"I have an early morning, so I think it's time to call it a night," Gordon said, mirroring her thoughts. "Ryan, let's have a look at Patches before I leave."

Taylor watched Ryan sail by; then a moment later a tail-wagging bundle of energy joined him in the kitchen. The dog seemed fine. In fact, it was adorable. She'd always had a fondness for dogs, especially Gordon's Max. Maybe someday she'd settle down in one place long enough to have one of her own.

She followed Ryan to the living room, where Priscilla was already pulling on her sweater and retrieving her car keys from her purse. Surviving an evening with Gordon, Sue, and Priscilla was nothing less than a miracle. Taylor gave herself a mental pat on the back.

And let out a silent sigh of relief.

"Hey, you're looking good, Patches," Gordon said, dropping to his knees to peer into the dog's eyes. He scratched Patches behind the ears, and the mutt seemed to melt into the floor at Gordon's feet. "Like that, huh, boy?"

He chuckled, sounding far too much like the boy Taylor had once adored. She loved hearing him laugh. She always had. That ache commenced again in her chest and her belly did a triple spinach lasagna flip. Her gaze rested on Gordon's silver hair, pulled into a ponytail at his nape. His face and neck were bronze from the sun, and the muscles in his forearms rippled beneath his blue-and-white rugby shirt.

"No more wheezing since he came home?" Straightening, Gordon looked at Ryan and Sue for his answer.

"Not a bit." Ryan beamed as he dropped to the floor beside his dog, whose tail swept the wood floor in rhythmic strokes. "He's well now. I think he likes the warmer weather."

"We all like the warmer weather." Gordon stroked his chin and nodded. "I hope he stays that way, but call me right away if he starts wheezing again."

"He won't," Ryan said, burying his face in the dog's furry neck. "Will you, Patch?"

"Will do, Gordon," Sue said, moving toward the door. "Thanks."

Taylor followed Gordon to the door. "Thank you for dinner, Sue. It was delicious."

Sue met her gaze and her smile was sad. "I hope you'll come again sometime, Taylor. It's good to have you home."

Taylor's belly did a number on the salad, and she gave a noncommittal nod. "Good night to you all."

"Good night, dear," Priscilla said. "Gordon, you

take Taylor straight home, and none of that parking you two used to do along the way. She's a doctor now."

Gordon's cheeks blazed as he reached for the doorknob, and Taylor swallowed her grin. She should be embarrassed, but watching him blush freed her to enjoy the moment.

She followed him down the sidewalk and slid into the passenger seat of his Jeep, allowing her fingertip to trail along the seat cover. Visions of the past forced their way out of the mental vault where she'd tried to lock them away. She and Gordon had spent so much time in this old Jeep. Her face warmed as she recalled some of their more intimate moments.

Glancing up, she noticed the way the floodlight bathed his silver hair as he walked around the front of the Jeep. A shiver chased itself through her that had nothing to do with air temperature. Gordon was her first love, and—God help her—her only love. What she felt for Jeremy could hardly be called love. Yet.

The wine she'd consumed mingled with desire and warmed her from within. She leaned against the seat with a sigh.

"Comfy?" he asked, sliding in and firing up the engine. It sputtered a few times, then roared to life. *"Good* car." He patted the steering wheel, and Taylor giggled.

"I think your Jeep is developing Alzheimer's."

He revved the engine and glowered at her. "Sometimer's."

She laughed and fastened her seat belt. "Okay, Sometimer's, then. It is getting old, huh?"

Gordon sighed and nodded in the semidarkness. "I'm afraid so. I sure hate to part with her, though."

"Her?"

He looked away and buckled his seat belt, then dropped the Jeep into reverse. "Of course. Ships are always her, aren't they? You don't remember helping me name her?"

"Oh . . ." Taylor swallowed hard. "Henrietta."

"Right, Henrietta." Silence enveloped them in a cocoon so private, Taylor could hear the thud of her own heart. Riding slowly through the small town in Gordon's Jeep brought a flood of reminiscing to the surface. Exhaustion and wine had lowered her defenses, and as they passed Al's Dog-n-Malt, her eyes stung and blurred.

"We sure ate our share of onion rings and french fries there," Gordon said, stopping at the only traffic signal in town.

"It's a miracle our arteries didn't clog before graduation." Taylor smiled to herself and turned her gaze on the dark silhouette of the man beside her. "It was nice to see your mother again. She looks good."

"Mom has the constitution of a twelve-year-old and never lets me forget it." He chuckled, then sighed. "It was hard on her when Dad died, though."

"I'm sorry. I didn't know."

"Of course you didn't." He looked right at her in the darkness. "You ran away."

"I—" She bit her lip to silence her retort. It was

true, after all. She had run away, but for a very good reason. How dared he blame it all on her? "I think you know why I left, Gordon, so let's stop pretending you don't."

"Do I?" The light turned green and Gordon eased the Jeep into motion. A barricade loomed before them, blocking Digby Boulevard. The street was flooded with water, and several uniformed men were working on the problem. "Looks like a broken water main. We'll have to skirt around the edge of town to get to your place."

"Don't change the subject." Taylor folded her arms across her abdomen and searched for the right words. "You *know* why I left."

Gordon drove in silence down the narrow county road that circled about a mile into the country. Eventually, it would horseshoe back to the far end of town.

There were no other vehicles on the road, and a half-moon hung in the sky, as if it had been painted on black velvet. She had forgotten how bright the moon and stars were at nine thousand feet above sea level.

But watching the stars couldn't prevent her irritation at Gordon's prolonged silence. "Gordon Lane, you *know* why I left," she repeated without looking at him.

He hit the brakes so hard, she was thrown against the seat belt and shoulder strap. "What—"

"A deer."

She turned to see the buck staring into the headlights. Gordon tapped the horn lightly. The deer vaulted into the trees.

She faced Gordon, prepared to confront him again. Just as she opened her mouth, Henrietta sputtered and rumbled, then fell silent.

"Uh-oh," he said.

"Uh-oh?"

"Could be the carburetor again. I'll have a look." He set the brake, then unfolded himself from the Jeep and raised the hood. The headlights and the moon were his only light.

Taylor dug through her bag and removed her penlight. It wasn't much, but it might help. Besides, she needed to get home and away from Gordon's charm immediately. Yesterday, in fact.

Determined to extricate herself from this situation immediately, she climbed from the vehicle and walked around to the front. She flashed her penlight. "Tell me where to point this thing."

He turned to stare at her and she aimed it at his face. His grin was infectious and she returned it. "All right, just find my hands," he said.

She located his hands in the engine and aimed the narrow beam there. "How's that?"

"A little lower. Perfect." He tinkered with the whatever-it-was, then sidled closer to her. "I need a different angle. See where I'm working?"

Taylor squinted and reached over Gordon's back to aim the light from the opposite side. Unfortunately, she was practically draped over him. "I'll move to the other side."

"No, I've almost got it." His voice crawled around inside her and did the tango.

She could barely breathe with her breasts pressed against his muscular back. Her heart slammed against her ribs so hard she suspected he felt it, too. Warmth oozed through her, pooling low and deliberately between her legs.

Her nipples hardened and her breasts swelled against him. Perspiration trickled down the sides of her neck and a cool mountain breeze soughed through the pines and made her shiver.

"Are you . . . almost finished?" she asked, her voice unnaturally husky.

"Yeah." He sounded gruff and out of breath as he backed away from the vehicle, freeing Taylor from her duty.

Cool air rushed across her breasts, which had been so very warm a moment ago. The contrast transformed her nipples into twin compass needles seeking magnetic north.

Gordon faced her, moonlight gleaming off his hair in patterns of brilliant silver as he reached out to brush the backs of his fingers against her cheek. She sighed and closed her eyes for an instant as remembrance deepened her physical and emotional response. She tried to summon the image of Jeremy's face but drew a blank. So much for "practically engaged."

"Thanks for helping," he whispered, dropping his hand to his side.

"You're welcome."

"But I think you should know something, Taylor."

*He must've noticed.* . . . "Wh-what?" She swallowed hard, preparing herself for humiliation.

He grinned, his white teeth flashing in the moonlight. "I finished about the time you offered to move."

# FIVE

The remembered heat of Taylor's body against his filled Gordon's dreams. Her nipples boring into his shoulder blades while he worked on the engine had driven him crazy. Unfortunately, that small sample had only whetted his appetite, so dreams of the summer between their junior and senior years in high school provided the balance of his torture.

One incident in particular replayed again and again on Morpheus's VCR. Their first time. God, he would never forget that afternoon. They'd been dating for almost a year by then, and necking in the backseat of his Jeep had grown daring enough to involve total nudity.

What happened next was a rite of passage.

Gordon had known it would happen. They both had. Fourth of July. The fireworks display in Digby couldn't come close to competing with what had happened earlier that day in Silas Canyon. He remembered every delectable detail. . . .

Taylor met him at Spring Park with a picnic basket; then they drove up to the canyon to eat by the waterfall. Amazingly, he even remembered her clothes—a pair of white shorts with a red belt and a blue tank top for the holiday. Her dark hair was pulled into a high ponytail that bobbed when she walked, curls spiraling toward her cheeks.

From the moment he pulled the parking brake on his Jeep and cut the engine, making love with Taylor became inevitable. Destined. The picnic lunch was the farthest thing from both their minds. And hearts.

"Come on, Gordon." With sunlight shining through the pines, she jumped out of the Jeep and gave him an inviting smile that nearly killed him. She pulled the ribbon from her hair and let it cascade down her back. "Last one in's a rotten egg." Still watching him, she let her expression grew solemn as she pulled her tank top over her head and hung it over the open window. Her sandals landed in the seat, followed by her shorts and a pair of plain white panties.

Nothing had ever looked sexier than Taylor's panties on the front seat of his Jeep. Except for Taylor herself, and the come-hither expression in her eyes.

Even at seventeen she had the shape of a woman. She looked like a wood nymph or some kind of goddess standing there with her curves kissed by dappled sunshine. They'd talked about going all the way, and now it looked as if it would finally happen.

Gordon's young body stood at attention. Every muscle tensed and his hands trembled as he pulled his T-shirt over his head. Watching Taylor walk toward him, he pulled off his sneakers and tube socks and tossed them into the Jeep with his shirt. By the time she paused in front of him, he wore only his cutoffs and briefs, and the biggest hard-on of his young life.

She placed both hands on his shoulders and stepped closer, the pink tips of her breasts brushing against his rib cage. He was dizzy, crazed, mad with desire.

"Kiss me, Gordon," she whispered, rising on tiptoe to meet his lips.

His arms went around her and she opened her mouth for his tongue. The only sexual experience they had was with each other, and they'd spent a lot of time practicing for this day. He knew how to kiss her, where to touch her. And he loved her with all his heart. Nothing was as important to him as Taylor. Nothing.

He buried his fingers in her silky hair as he tasted her. Her arms went around his neck and she trembled against him, her nipples flattened against his chest. Slowly, he eased his hands down her back, relishing her softness, savoring her bare skin. Emboldened, he cupped her bare bottom and pressed her hips against his.

She pulled back, her lips red and swollen, her green eyes drugged with passion. Then a wicked smile curved her mouth and she bolted for the falls, giggling all the way.

Breathless, Gordon stripped off his remaining clothing, grabbed his Indiana Jones beach towel, then chased after her, only somewhat self-conscious about his nudity and his blatant erection. Taylor had seen that part of him—touched him there—before. Even so, he was more aware of his engorged state today than ever.

What would it be like inside her? He stumbled at the thought, remembering the hot slickness of his tongue in her mouth. Warm. Wet. Wonderful.

Taylor shrieked as she slipped behind the cold sheet of water pouring down the canyon wall. Even in midsummer, the water up here was frigid. He slowed his pace on the slippery rocks and ducked beneath an outcropping, then emerged behind the falls.

With Taylor.

A cool mist surrounded them, and the roar of the water spilling to the creek below created a world all their own. They were as isolated as two people could be. Together.

The cold spray from the falls did nothing to diminish his enthusiasm. In fact, the water enhanced the erotic urges pulsing through him. His gaze feasted on the sight of her standing there, her bare flesh damp and glistening, her eyes wide with wonder as she looked at him. All of him.

They didn't speak as they came together, all mouths, hands, gasping, kneading. His erection pressed against her lower abdomen, aching, throbbing, wanting. He dropped the beach towel to the damp stone, then eased her down. She held her arms up to him invitingly.

Gordon thought once, briefly, of the condoms in his glove compartment, until she rose up on her knees and took him in her hands. Gazing upward, her expression banished further thought of anything even remotely practical.

Fearing he would lose control, he reached down and grasped her wrists, pulling her hands away. He kissed her mouth, suckled the lobe of her ear, still holding her hands in both of his out to their sides.

Her breasts thrust upward, rising and falling with her rapid breathing. For a few minutes, all he could do was look at her, vowing to never forget a single precious detail.

She reached for him and he kissed her again, wild and deep. Cupping her breasts in his hands, he lowered his mouth to her nipple, drawing her deeply into his mouth. So soft. So sweet. She moaned and arched against him, and he hungrily sampled her other breast.

"Make love to me, Gordon," she whispered.

He rose onto his elbows and met her gaze. "Are you sure? Very sure?"

"I don't think Indiana Jones will mind." An impish grin curved her full lips. "Don't you want to?"

"More than anything. You know that." He kissed her again, dipping his fingers into her honeyed core, knowing the time had come. He'd read an article in *Playboy* about how to get a woman ready for sex. The article had suggested that a man use his mouth, but he wasn't sure either of them was ready for that just yet. Instead, he sought and found the small nub between her thighs and rotated it with the pad of his finger. Her response was more than he'd dreamed. She moaned and pushed herself upward against his hand.

As desperately as he wanted this, he was determined to make it as wonderful for Taylor as he knew it would be for him. She cried out his name and her body went stiff for a few silent moments.

"That was . . ."

"Did I hurt you?" he asked.

Her eyes were half closed as she reached for him, shaking her head. "Wonderful."

"I . . ." He looked down at himself, the red tip of his penis ready and waiting. "I . . ."

She reached for him, wrapping her fingers around his shaft. "Now."

A shudder of anticipation and apprehension rippled through him as she guided him to her soft folds. She was slick and wet and hot, and it was all he could do to prevent himself from plunging deep and hard and fast.

She eased her legs behind his and held him against her, easing him into her one torturous millimeter at a time. Gordon held his breath, allowing her to set the pace.

Her expression was a cross between wonder and pain. He'd heard it was always painful for a woman the first time. "I . . . I think I have to push harder now."

She nodded and bit her lower lip.

"Taylor." He held himself back and kissed her, then stared deeply into her eyes, summoning his courage. "We can stop now . . . if you want." *Even if it kills me.*

She shook her head and wrapped her legs around

him tighter, drawing him inward. "I want you to do it."

He buried himself inside her, aware of something hot and wet running between them. Pleasure like he'd never known before coiled within him, urging him to drive into her again and again, but he held himself frozen and searched her eyes. "Did I hurt you?" He could barely breathe, let alone speak.

"A little." She wrapped her arms around his neck. "But it's better now."

Better was a weak word to describe what he felt with his body buried deeply inside Taylor's. Ecstasy came close, but still couldn't do this miracle justice. She clung to him as he stroked the length of her, urging him to move harder and faster. The muscles inside her massaged and held him, torturing him with the promise of something he could barely imagine.

Everything he had culminated where their bodies were joined. A molten rush exploded from him and he stiffened and spasmed against and into her.

Breathless and dripping with sweat, he slumped over her. "Wow." Bracing his hands on either side of her, he looked down and saw tears in her eyes. "I hurt you."

She shook her head and buried her face against his chest. "I just love you so much," she murmured. "So much it scares me."

"I love you, too." He stood and held his hand out to her, recognizing the significance of what they'd just shared. A woman only gave herself once this way. He could never return what she'd given him today, and it was a gift he would always cherish.

Afterward, he bathed her in the creek as the sun slowly sank behind the mountain. Then they dressed and drove back to town for the fireworks, vowing to always love one another.

No matter what . . .

Gordon awoke with a start, sunlight streaming through the slats on his shutters. He glanced down at the tented sheet and realized that he needed his ritual swim for more reasons than one this morning. Raking his fingers through his hair, he padded barefoot to his closet and retrieved a large box from the top shelf.

Carefully, he set it on his bed and lifted the lid, revealing an envelope of photos—all of Taylor—and a piece of ribbon she'd worn in her hair. Then he folded back the tissue paper to reveal the old beach towel. He'd washed it, then put it away after that afternoon with Taylor, vowing never to use it again.

The bittersweet ache spread through his chest as he refolded the towel and returned it to his closet. This simple beach towel had become a treasure, and his recollection of that summer afternoon was permanent.

Taylor's love was not.

* * *

Taylor checked the contents of her medical bag. With the box of supplies she'd left at the clinic the day before, she should be all set to begin her medical career. She grabbed one more slug of coffee, then headed out the back door to her VW.

Before she reached the car, an eerie pricking sensation crept up the back of her neck. Slowing her pace, she looked around the backyard, expecting to find someone watching her. When she saw no one, she laughed it off and continued toward the car.

All the gravel on the drive had washed away over the years, leaving bare dirt in its place. She noticed the prints immediately. Bear prints.

Her heart pressed against her throat and she held her breath. An icy chill swooped through her body. Her forehead went numb, her lips tingled, terror gripped her.

She was ten again and hiding in an abandoned shack from a wounded bear. The beast had spotted her when she lagged behind the other Girl Scouts and chased her to the inadequate shelter. Growling and snarling, the bear had tried to push the building down while Taylor screamed and prayed with all her might, until the Girl Scout leader and all the parents and girls had made enough noise to drive the bear away.

And now there were bear tracks around her car. In town.

Her gaze darted around the yard again, over her shoulder; then she bolted for the car and slammed the door. Inside, she rested her forehead against the steering wheel, waiting for her breathing to return to normal.

It wasn't unheard of for bears to come down into town this time of year, usually foraging through garbage cans and draining hummingbird feeders. Tonight, she would park her car in front of the house. Closer to the door. And she'd stop at the hardware store and get a new sensor for the motion detector. That would help.

Her sanity slowly returned and she started the car, then backed out of the drive. So far, her stay in Digby had been one disaster after another, and she'd barely begun her three-year tour of duty. Well, she couldn't exactly call dinner a disaster. All things considered, it had gone rather well.

Except for that incident out on Vista Road . . .

Heat flooded her cheeks as she dropped the car into first, then started down the hill toward Drumond Avenue and the clinic. And Gordon.

Warmth invaded more than her face as she remembered how her body had reacted to touching his last night. She rolled down the window, and the early morning air flowed through the tiny car, cooling her cheeks and the rest of her body within seconds.

"I can do this," she muttered, turning the corner onto Drumond. She dropped the car to a lower gear and crept toward the veterinary clinic. "I can do this."

Gritting her teeth, she swung the car into a parking space at the back of the building, beside Gordon's Jeep. She sat staring at Henrietta for several seconds; then she drew a deep breath, girded her resolve, and opened the door.

"I can do this. I *will* do this." Medical bag in tow, she used the key Gordon had given her to open the back door. Inside, she blinked and waited for her eyes to adjust to being out of the bright Rocky Mountain sunshine.

" 'Morning, Taylor," Sue called, buzzing down the hallway in high gear. "Gordon's in surgery most of the morning."

"Good morning." How could anyone move that fast this early? *Ryan must've gotten it from his mother.* Taylor needed more coffee; then she'd have to talk to Sue about the logistics of getting her patients back to her exam room. She would also need to pay Sue something for all the extra work. After all, she was a single mother.

That part still confused Taylor, but she refused to think about it now. Today, she had to play doctor for real. She stowed her medical bag in what would pass as her office for now, then went in search of the coffeepot she'd spotted yesterday. The aroma reached her long before she found it. She removed a cup from a hook and filled it with the rich brown liquid, reminding herself to bring her insulated mug tomorrow so she'd have something with a lid.

Taking a long sip, she leaned against the counter for a moment and remembered what Sue had said a few minutes ago. If Gordon was in surgery all morning, then he probably wouldn't have a waiting room full of furry, four-footed patients scheduled. Maybe she would have one of her own. Or two.

Though this type of medicine wasn't what she really wanted to practice, she still wanted to be useful and busy. Plus, this was her first independent experience as a physician. She smiled and lifted her coffee cup in a mock toast to her first day on the job.

"Taylor, there you are." Sue popped her head around the corner. "We have an emergency." The woman vanished as quickly as she'd appeared, leaving Taylor no choice but to follow.

She saw Sue turn into one of the exam rooms, and Taylor raced down the hall after her, wondering why she hadn't put the patient in Taylor's office. Pausing in the doorway, she saw the reason. Approximately seventy-five pounds of golden fur were sprawled out on a stainless-steel table.

"Wha—"

"Is it bad?" a woman asked from across the room.

Taylor's gaze took in the woman's dark glasses, and she realized that the dog was this woman's eyes. "What happened?" She shoved up her sleeves and went to the patient, forgetting its species for now. As long as it wasn't a bear, she could handle it.

"She was trying to protect me," the woman sobbed. "There was a bro-broken window at the store."

Sue was still applying pressure to the animal's hind leg. "The dog put herself between her and the glass." Her eyes were moist and imploring when she looked up at Taylor. "She needs stitches, and Gordon's tied up for at least another hour."

"I . . ." Taylor looked from the woman to the

dog, then nodded. "Can you ask Gordon what to give the dog as a sedative and how much?"

Taylor placed her own hand over the gauze pad on the dog's wound, amazed at how still and quiet the animal was. "Good girl," she said, telling herself that stitching up a dog's leg was no different from stitching up a hairy human one. She'd have Sue help her shave a little fur away; then they'd take care of the injury. "What's her name?"

"Goldie," the owner said. "I'm Sally Bradshaw."

"Are you related to the mayor?"

"Tom is my brother. I live with his family."

Taylor pulled a corner of the gauze away and peeked. Sue was right about the stitches. The glass had sliced a deep gash that wouldn't stop bleeding on its own. The dog flinched and whimpered when she reapplied the pressure but made no effort to rise. "You can go stand by Goldie's head if you wish, Sally."

The woman rose from her chair and felt her way along the wall to the table, then rested her hands on Goldie's head. "There's my girl," she cooed.

Taylor's first patient might be a dog, but in many ways Sally was also her patient. Goldie was Sally's eyes and she was injured. In a roundabout way, she was treating a human.

"I think she's going to be fine, Sally," Taylor said. "Once we get this wound stitched and the bleeding stopped, it will be a matter of making sure she doesn't get an infection."

"That's good." Sally stroked the dog's head. "She's very healthy."

"I can see that, which is why I'm confident she'll be all right."

"Is . . . is her leg damaged?"

"I can't be entirely certain there's no soft tissue damage, but time will tell." Taylor drew a deep breath. "We can take an X ray to make sure there are no broken bones, too, though that's unlikely with this type of injury."

"Thank you, Doctor."

"You're welcome." And she was.

Sue came in with a metal tray that included a filled syringe and everything necessary to stitch the wound. A short time later, the dog was dozing, the wound bandaged, and Sally sat in her chair right beside the exam table, her hand resting on Goldie's neck.

Taylor pulled off her gloves and dropped them into the red container in the corner. She met Sue's gaze and the woman nodded. "You done good, Doc."

Satisfaction eased through Taylor, along with something she hadn't felt since high school: a bond with Sue Wheeler. "Thanks. So did you."

"I'd like to stay here with Goldie," Sally said.

"Sure," Sue said. "I called your brother, and he'll be here any minute."

"Thank you," Sally said.

"I'd like to have Gordon look at her before you take her home anyway, and make sure the sedative has worn off." Taylor didn't doubt her ability at stitching simple wounds, but Goldie was a canine, after all.

"Looks to me like you have things well in hand, Doctor."

The male voice startled Taylor and her breath caught. She swallowed hard and met Gordon's approving gaze. "Thanks."

"Dr. Lane, Dr. Bowen saved Goldie's life."

"I'm glad she was here for you, Sally," Gordon said, his voice quiet, his gaze continuing to hold Taylor's.

Sue cleared her throat and slipped behind Gordon. "I'd better go check messages and see if anyone is in the waiting room."

Gordon glanced at the bandage and gave Taylor a thumbs-up gesture. "Everything looks fine, Sally," he said. "I'll have to send her home in a cone collar so she won't be able to chew the stitches."

"All right. Thanks."

"I need to get back to my office now and finish setting things up," Taylor said, wanting desperately to escape. Gordon's approval felt too good and meant too much to her. It shouldn't. It couldn't.

"I'm leaving the door open, Sally," Gordon said, putting his hand on Taylor's arm. "The minute you feel or hear Goldie waking, you call out and one of us will come running. Okay? And I'll have Sue bring you a soda. Dr Pepper, right?"

"Thanks. I'd like that."

Taylor was trapped. Gordon shifted his hand from her arm to the small of her back and steered her from the room, giving Sue the instructions he'd just mentioned to Sally as they passed the reception desk and headed toward Taylor's new office.

Bewildered, Taylor found herself in her office with the door closed and Gordon's arms around her before she drew her next breath. He gazed deeply into her eyes, then lowered his mouth to hers.

Her momentary shock gave way to a cascade of joy. His kiss was deep and wet and thorough, and she returned it with far too much enthusiasm. He tasted as sweet now as he had ten years ago, and her heart swelled with something she refused to identify.

Suddenly, he released her, and she swayed to keep her balance, staring stupidly up into his glittering turquoise eyes. "Why?" she whispered, not sure if she'd been kissed or punished.

"I had to see if it was the way I remembered."

Her belly flip-flopped and she drew a sharp breath. "Was it?" Not that she should care . . .

He sighed and reached for the doorknob. "Better."

The tone of his voice made it clear that he was disappointed with the results of his test. Taylor lifted her chin and struggled against the urge to throw herself into his arms. Her nose and throat burned, but her stubbornness wouldn't permit the tears to flow.

He jerked open the door and closed it quietly behind him. Taylor rested her cheek against the cool surface and squeezed her eyes shut.

*Oh, yes. Much better.*

# SIX

Gordon rubbed his temples, sensing what was about to erupt. Sue had that look—the one that spelled L-E-C-T-U-R-E. The infuriating thing about Sue's lectures was that she was almost always right. *Dammit.*

"Taylor just left." Sue placed her palms on his desk and leaned toward him. "She's been here over a week. You *have* to talk to her, Gordon."

*Yeah, almost always right, but not this time.* He summoned a bland expression and grabbed a pencil to occupy his hands, twirling it between his thumbs and forefingers. "I have talked to her. Every day."

"About . . . what happened?" Sue's face paled. "You told her everything?"

Gordon closed his eyes, remembering. "No, we haven't discussed that." He met Sue's gaze. "And we aren't going to. It's over, Sue. Let it go."

She shook her head very slowly. "You're lying to yourself, buddy. It's far from over."

Gordon's gut twisted into a knot and the pencil snapped in two. "Don't go there, Sue." His voice dropped to a whisper. "Just . . . don't." His dreams provided enough ongoing torture to send him to an early grave. He didn't need this.

She stared at him as if trying to read his mind. "You have to talk to her." Her expression softened. "Gordon, I've seen the way you two look at each other. The sexual tension in this place is so thick you could—"

"Stop."

Sue smacked the desk with the flat of her palm. "No, I won't stop." She closed her eyes and drew a shaky breath, then gave him an imploring look. "It's all my fault, Gordon. Mine." Her lower lip trembled. "I can't undo the past, but I can try to do something about the future. I have to. This is k-killing me."

"Ah, hell, don't cry." He raked his fingers through his hair, then stood and walked around the desk. "Come here, you." He pulled her into his arms. "It isn't your fault. Taylor knew what she was doing when she walked out on me." A fresh onslaught of pain stabbed through him. "She didn't trust me. I can't forgive that. It's over. Let it rest. I have." *What a crock.*

Sue pushed away and met his gaze, tears trickling down her cheeks. "I've lived with this guilt for ten years, Gordon. *Ten years.*"

"You don't have t—"

"Yes, I do." She bit her lower lip and sniffled. "It's my fault she left and we both know it."

"If she'd trusted me . . ."

"Why does that matter now?" Sue's lips trembled again. "She was hurt and confused. That's why she left—the *only* reason she left, and we both know it. Because of me . . ."

"Don't cry." Gordon pulled her against his shoulder again. "Please, don't cry anymore."

"Will you talk to her?" Sue pulled back again, pinning him with her gaze. "Will you?"

"I don't know." Gordon rubbed her upper arms and swallowed the bile burning his throat like battery acid. Taylor had tried to talk about the past that night the Jeep died out on Vista Road. He didn't want to dredge it up again. Ever. It hurt too damned much. "Not yet. Maybe. I don't know."

"Think about it." A threatening tremor entered her voice. "Please?"

Gordon remained silent for several seconds, staring beyond Sue and into the past. "I said I'll think about it," he promised. As if he could stop thinking of Taylor. She occupied his thoughts every spare moment and then some these days.

But there was an important point Sue had overlooked. "Has it occurred to you . . . ?"

"What?" Sue sniffled again.

"That *you're* the one who should talk to her?"

Sue's eyes widened. She pulled out of his embrace and paced the room. "Me?" She paused, biting her fingernail. "I don't know if she'd listen to me after—"

"What makes you think she'd listen to me?" With a sigh, he tossed the broken pencil onto the desk and watched both halves roll until they came to a stop against the telephone. "It's late. Go home."

"You said you'd think about it."

"Trust me, I will." He gritted his teeth. "How's Patches doing?"

"A little wheezing last night, and I'm starting to think Ryan's right about the weather causing this. It was colder last night." Her brow furrowed. "Aren't those test results due back from UNC?"

"Yeah, I'll give them a call tomorrow and get a verbal." He rubbed his chin, thankful he'd managed to change the subject, but sorry to hear that Ryan's dog was ill again. "Call me if he gets any worse, and have Ryan bring him by tomorrow after school. That mutt is an enigma."

"He isn't the only one." Sue grabbed her sweater and purse from the chair where she'd left them when she first stormed into Gordon's office. "I expect you to think about talking to Taylor. You promised." She pulled on her sweater and retrieved her keys from her purse. "You're too stubborn to admit it, but you're still crazy about each other."

"Ancient hist—"

"Later." Sue waggled her fingers over her shoulder and headed for the back door in overdrive.

"She always gets the last word," he muttered, throwing his hands into the air and shaking his head. Women. He'd never understand the creatures. Even his mother had softened her heart toward Taylor, inviting her to join church and community activities.

Which reminded him that he was due at City Hall this evening for a town council meeting. He glanced at his watch. "So much for dinner." After grabbing his jacket, he left last-minute instructions with Hank, the retired truck driver who worked nights at the clinic, then headed for his Jeep with barely enough time to make the meeting.

A few minutes later, he parked outside City Hall, the only three-story building in town, and bounded up the old stone steps. The meeting hall was packed. Odd. These meetings were usually sparsely attended unless something controversial was on the agenda.

He sure as hell hoped they weren't resurrecting that limited-stakes gambling issue. That would be the end of the small town he knew and loved. Legalizing gambling had irrevocably changed Cripple Creek. As long as he served on the Digby Town Council, he'd fight to prevent that from happening here. Fortunately, most citizens shared his feelings.

Even the women's circle from church was here, with cookies and punch. Something was definitely going on. He grabbed a cookie off a passing tray and shoved it into his mouth, ignoring his mother's arched eyebrow as he sped by.

"Ah, there he is," Mayor Bradshaw said as Gordon hurried toward his chair at the head table. "Running a little late?"

"Sorry, Tom," Gordon said, sliding into his chair. He nodded to the other three council members. Everybody in town seemed to be here tonight. Had he been so preoccupied that he'd forgotten something important?

"This meeting will now come to order." Tom banged his gavel, taking his role much too seriously. "It's nice to see such a big crowd here to welcome our new doctor."

*Taylor.* Sighing, Gordon rubbed the back of his neck and wondered how he could've forgotten this.

Of course, the reason for his distraction was also the reason for this gathering.

"Since I only came to Digby five years ago, I didn't realize Dr. Bowen was a local girl." Tom chuckled. "But some of you have told me enough stories about her growing up here that I almost feel as if I knew her then."

*Mom.* Gordon wished he could slide under the table.

"Dr. Bowen graduated from Digby High School with honors," Tom continued. "She lettered in softball, was president of the science club, and served on the high school debate team. . . ."

*She's still good at that.* Gordon tuned out Tom's speech and scanned the crowd. Taylor sat in the front row with her legs crossed at the knees. A dark green dress hung from her shoulders to her belted waist, then fell in soft folds almost to her ankles. She'd gone home to change after work. Her hair curled around her shoulders. This was the first time he'd seen it down since her return.

She looked good enough to eat.

Musical notes drifted to him from the piano at the end of the riser, jerking Gordon's attention away from the woman who'd turned his life topsy-turvy. Mrs. Johnson had dragged herself away from Precious long enough to play for the women's choir from the First—and only—Congregational Church.

As the singers lapsed into their third number, Gordon stifled a yawn and turned his attention back to Taylor. Her eyes widened and their gazes held. She'd been watching him, too. *Busted.* Well, he was as guilty as she.

Her lips curved in a knowing smile, as potent as a gut punch. His body sprang to life, and he felt like the teenager he once was. He seemed predisposed to a state of constant arousal where Taylor Bowen was concerned.

His libido had no common sense whatsoever, but *he* sure as hell did—or better. Just because he couldn't keep his hormones in check around her didn't mean he had to follow through with his impulses. Though the thought of following through elevated the state of his male anatomy to dire and dangerous.

Okay, desperate.

Other than Meghan, a fairly long-term relationship after he'd returned from college to set up his practice, Gordon's love life hadn't amounted to much. He'd been unable to commit himself to marriage, and that's what she'd wanted. Now married to the high school football coach, Meghan had it all, with one child and another on the way.

Then he'd proposed to Sue, who'd laughed and told him she wasn't into incest. Okay, so they weren't related, but she was right—any relationship beyond friendship would've been too weird for words. After that, Gordon had resumed his life as a semirecluse and veterinarian.

And the reason he hadn't been able to commit to Meghan sat in the front row of City Hall. *Taylor.* He shifted on the hard chair, his gaze still fixed on her. She licked her lips and he bit his own, remembering how she'd tasted when he grabbed and kissed her in his office last week.

*Damn.*

The high school band filed into the hall at the rear and the choir members left the stage. Gordon forced his attention away from Taylor. The band marched up the center aisle playing something Gordon couldn't even begin to identify, and he felt certain no one else could either. They paused in front of the riser, facing the audience, and completed their number. The crowd applauded and the mayor took the podium again.

"Dr. Bowen, on behalf of all the citizens of Digby, Colorado"—he smiled like he was up for reelection—"welcome home."

*Home?* Taylor's throat convulsed and her belly churned. The mayor called her to the stage and she allowed her gaze to sweep the crowd as she stood at his side. So many familiar faces. Amazing, considering how long she'd been gone. A strange ache commenced in her heart. This whole mess was something like finding a long-lost sweater and trying it on to learn it still fit.

But Digby didn't fit—rather, she didn't fit.

The mayor pumped her hand and stepped aside, indicating that she should take the microphone. Drawing a deep breath, she slipped behind the podium and lowered the microphone to her level.

"Thank you all for the wonderful welcome." She resisted the word *home,* though it lingered in her mind, refusing to be completely banished despite her best efforts. All eyes looked at her expectantly, and she suddenly realized that she couldn't deny her roots. These people knew her, and they liked being able to claim her as one of their own. After all, she'd been born and raised here. Fallen in love here . . .

"When I was a little girl, we had a doctor," she continued. "I imagine most of you remember Dr. Eddington." Many heads nodded and a murmur swept through the crowd. "When I was nine, he treated me for a broken collarbone after I went over the handlebars of my bike. That was when I decided to become a doctor."

All true. A deluge of memories flooded her and she drew another fortifying breath. Public speaking was bad enough by itself, but it was beyond cruel to have to face all the ghosts of her past—including Gordon—at the same time.

"And it's also why I've asked Mayor Bradshaw to name the clinic after Dr. Eddington." Applause and cheers erupted, and Taylor waited. "Whenever it opens." More laughter, and she took that opportunity to glare at the mayor, whose face was as red as the carnation in his lapel. Gordon sat beside Tom Bradshaw, his expression unreadable, his appearance breathtaking. Straightening, she faced the crowd again, finding many expectant faces less unnerving than Gordon's one.

"Again, I thank you for this wonderful welcome." She stepped aside, but the mayor indicated that she should take his chair. Beside Gordon. Bolting for her vacant seat in the front row now would look pretty cowardly, so she gave a tight smile and perched herself on the edge of the chair.

Where Gordon Lane was concerned, she was like a heat-seeking missile. Despite the foot or so that separated their chairs, she *felt* his warmth at her side. She cast a furtive glance from the corner of her eye and found him watching her, his eyes hooded, his brow furrowed.

Sympathy—no, empathy—washed through her. He hadn't asked her to invade his life again, after all. Perhaps it was time to tell him about Jeremy and her career plans. That might help them both put things into perspective.

Jeremy Cole was a young doctor from a wealthy Philadelphia family. His parents liked her, despite her humble lineage. If she accepted Jeremy's proposal, she'd go to Philadelphia and never have to worry about money again.

But could she marry a man she didn't really love? She *liked* him well enough, but not the way—

With a mental groan, she looked at Gordon again. He had his arms folded across his abdomen, and one corner of his mouth quirked upward in a manner that made her wonder if he'd been reading her mind.

She faced forward, unable to follow the mayor's speech. *Think about Jeremy.* Closing her eyes for a moment, she conjured his face. He was a hunk, but in a too-pretty way—not rugged and bronzed like Gordon.

Hissing softly to herself for allowing her thoughts to stray to Gordon again, she opened her eyes. *Jeremy. Focus, Taylor. Jeremy . . .*

A sinking feeling smacked her in the belly.

*Jeremy who?*

* * *

Sue padded around her kitchen hours after she'd tucked Ryan and Patches into bed. She should've gone to the welcoming ceremony for Taylor, but it would've been too late for Ryan to be up on a school night.

With a pink terry-cloth robe tied around her waist and fuzzy slippers with wiggly eyes keeping her feet toasty, she plopped into a chair at the kitchen table with a cup of herbal tea and a deck of tarot cards. She lit a yellow candle and placed it in the center of the table.

Somehow, she *would* get Gordon and Taylor together again. The question was . . . how? Any fool could see that they were soul mates, and it was all her fault that they weren't together.

A problem she intended to rectify, no matter what.

She looked at the deck and opened the instruction book. All right, so she was an amateur, but she was a desperate amateur. "I'm trainable," she muttered, shuffling the deck at least three times as the booklet said.

Concentrating on Gordon and Taylor, she cut the deck. The instructions for a Celtic cross spread lay before her, and she followed them to the letter, but no matter how many times she referred to the book, she didn't understand what it all meant.

"Something simpler." She leafed through the book and came to a single card reading. "Simple enough."

The instructions said to shuffle, concentrate on the question, cut the deck, then draw one card. "Okay, even I can do that." If she only had to decipher the meaning of one card, maybe she could learn something constructive here.

"Tell me the secret to getting Gordon and Taylor together," she whispered, following the instructions. The card she drew was the Moon, featuring a drawing of the moon with a face in it, and wolves howling at it from below.

"Okay, so what does *that* mean?" She leafed through the booklet and found the explanation of the card. " 'Error, sudden danger, illusion; instinct and portent are significant and beneficial, so the querist should heed them; commence with prudence.' "

Rolling her eyes, she said, "Right, something definitely isn't as it seems—Taylor and Gordon." The cards were a waste of time. She put the deck back in the box with the booklet and took a sip of her tea. She needed something concrete.

Rising, she blew out the candle and headed for the door. With a sigh, she turned out the light, then made her way down the hall to peek in at Ryan. He was snoring softly, his arm draped across the hairy mutt he loved so much. She smiled to herself, then went to her bedroom.

The full moon shone through the lace curtains like a spotlight, illuminating her bed. "Well, duh." She smacked herself in the forehead. "That's it."

All she had to do was get Gordon and Taylor in bed together. Nature would handle the rest.

\* \* \*

Taylor lingered with the townspeople long enough to be polite, then made her excuses and headed for the door. She needed to put some distance between herself and the past. Thankfully, she hadn't seen Gordon since shortly after the meeting had ended and they vacated the head table.

And yet, God help her, she'd been searching for him in the crowd. This was all so unhealthy, not to mention unwise. She couldn't prevent herself from thinking about him. Constantly.

The night was chilly and she pulled her sweater closer, slinging the strap of her bag over her shoulder. She paused on the steps and drew a deep breath. It was deliciously quiet compared to the revelry inside. After drawing another appreciative breath of the crisp evening air, she headed down the stone steps toward her car.

"Free at last?" a voice asked from the darkness.

Her heart screeched to a halt and she tripped, but Gordon's strong arm snaked out to grab her around the waist. And pulled her right against his hard chest.

"You startled me," she whispered, staring up at his face, bathed in the glow from the moon.

"I'm sorry for that," he said, his voice rough and evocative, "but I'm not sorry I caught you."

Their hearts thudded along in unison. Though they stood on Digby Boulevard, they were alone. Completely alone.

"Gordon, I . . ." She swallowed hard, struggling for words. She should push away from him and run to her car. *No, I will not run again.*

"I'm confused," he said quietly, still holding her. "Why did you come home, Taylor?"

"I . . . you know why." She tried to draw a deep breath but found the effort futile. Instead, rapid breathing fulfilled her need for oxygen. "Gordon, please."

"Please what?" He lowered his head toward hers, and his hands were warm against her back as his lips found hers.

Shock gave way to a welcoming rush so powerful, she couldn't deny it. His tongue eased between her parted lips, and she forgot reason. She'd been starving for this. For Gordon.

God help her.

A giant crevice opened beneath her feet and in her heart, swallowing her whole. Suffocating her. She wanted his wonderful mouth on all of her. She wanted *him*.

He deepened the kiss, fitting her more firmly against him as he tasted and plundered. Moaning, she grew acutely aware of how hard he was against her. And ready. Heated moisture pooled between her thighs, reminding her that he wasn't the only one ready.

He pivoted, and a cold stone pillar pressed against her back, contrasting startlingly with his hard heat. She almost sobbed when he cupped her bottom in his hands, suggesting that he had what she wanted. What she craved. He could slake her hunger so easily. So completely.

She clung to him, relishing the softness of his hair and the rigidness of his body. He brought his hand to her rib cage, brushing his thumb upward along the seam of her dress. Higher.

Her breasts strained against the confines of her bra, and her nipples hardened as he teased and tantalized. Then he cupped her breast in his hand, and her hips instinctively thrust toward him. Her muscles convulsed around the excruciating emptiness. She wanted—needed—him inside her.

More than that. She wanted and needed his gentleness. There was no man on earth as good or as loving as Gordon Lane. How could she have forgotten that?

He broke their kiss, gasping for breath. Befuddled, Taylor swayed as he stepped away, then grew aware of the massive doors opening as people started down the steps toward them.

"Come on." He grabbed her hand and tugged, leaving her no choice but to follow.

Next thing Taylor knew, she was settled in the front passenger seat of his Jeep, her breathing gradually returning to normal, though her body still burned. "What . . . ?" She turned to him. Within moments, their combined heat had the windows fogged over.

A low chuckle rumbled from his chest. "Brings back memories."

Taylor laughed, too, though she could barely contain the urge to invite him home with her. She longed to feel his hard length against her, pressing her into the mattress, filling the part of her that remained empty. Bereft.

After the crowds filed past, Gordon reached behind her and caressed the nape of her neck. A shiver raced down her spine and she never wanted him to stop touching her.

"Damn, what the hell are we doing?" He stiffened and pulled his hand away. She watched him grip the steering wheel as he stared straight ahead. Finally, he faced her. "I don't know what came over me," he said. "I'm sorry."

No, she didn't want his apology. She wanted *him*. "Sorry?"

"I shouldn't have . . ."

Weariness settled over her, chasing away the hunger. Temporarily. "No, I suppose not."

"I'll drive you home."

"I have my car." She reached for the door handle, relieved to see the sidewalk was empty. "I'll see you tomorrow."

Somehow, she managed to extricate herself from the Jeep and find her own car. A few moments later, she remembered that she needed gas. She stopped at the convenience store at the bottom of the hill and bought five dollars' worth of unleaded and a giant chocolate bar.

By the time she parked her car in front of her house, she'd eaten the entire bar. What they said about chocolate wasn't true, she realized, licking her fingers. It wasn't better than sex, but it was a fair substitute. For now.

With trembling hands, she unlocked and opened the door, then turned on the light. *Home.*

"No, not home."

The memory of Gordon's lips on hers sent a

shiver of longing down her spine even as it made her lift her chin in defiance. She wasn't staying in Digby, so allowing herself to get involved with Gordon Lane again would be a major mistake. It didn't matter how he made her feel, or what he made her want. It didn't matter that she'd once adored him.

She couldn't let it matter.

Drawing a deep breath, she picked up the phone and dialed Jeremy's number in Philadelphia. His mother answered.

"Taylor," she said excitedly, "how nice to hear from you. Jeremy's been worried."

"Hello, Mrs. Cole." *Cole, yes. Jeremy Cole.* Taylor dropped into the chair beside the phone, letting her purse hit the floor near her feet. "I've been busy getting settled. Sorry I didn't call sooner."

"Hold on. I'll get Jeremy."

She heard mumbling; then a strong male voice came across the line. "Taylor, thank God you're all right. I've been beside myself."

She drew another deep breath. "I'm sorry."

"I'm glad you called. Dad has business in Denver next week, and I'll be flying out with him on the company jet."

"Oh." She kicked off her shoes, trying to keep the unreasonable reluctance she felt from coming across in her tone. "This time of year is nice in Denver."

"Send me directions to Dugby and I'll rent a car."

"Digby, Jeremy."

"Whatever. Can you fax the directions tomorrow?"

"Sure." She bit her lower lip. Meeting Jeremy would put a stop to Gordon's interest in her—whatever that might be. "Yes, I'll do that first thing in the morning."

"I can't wait to see you," Jeremy said, his voice lowering. "I've missed you."

She blinked, wondering why she couldn't reciprocate his feelings. "It'll be good to see you again." That much was true. She liked Jeremy, even had a warm fondness for him.

"Have you talked to the mayor about buying out your contract?"

She winced. "No, I told you I don't want to—"

"Taylor, your talent is being wasted in that backwater town and you know it."

"But I feel responsible for—"

"Money talks." Jeremy's tone left no room for argument. "Trust me on this."

"You're forgetting that I don't *have* money, Jeremy."

"But I do." She heard him kiss the telephone. "Ciao."

" 'Bye."

She returned the phone to its cradle and flopped against the back of the chair. Yes, Jeremy would put a stop to Gordon's kisses.

And that was what she wanted. Wasn't it?

# SEVEN

Nothing was going right. First, that stupid bear stole Gordon's towel again; then his Jeep died on his way down the mountain. Again. To top it all off, he found his waiting room full and Sue in a mood he figured she'd blame on PMS or some other quirk of womanhood.

"Batting a thousand," he muttered as he checked his appointment book.

"Goldie's here to have her stitches removed," Sue said, her monthly scowl worse than usual.

"Bad night?" Gordon raised an eyebrow, realizing his error before the words even left his mouth. "Oops."

Sue swerved around to face him. "Living dangerously these days, Doctor?" An insidious smile spread itself across her face. "After Goldie, Precious *and* Mrs. Johnson are next on your agenda."

"You're like Dr. Jekyll and Ms. Hyde sometimes. You know that?"

"Ms. Hyde is armed, dangerous, and low on estrogen. Watch it." She batted her lashes. "Next thing you know, I'll be howling at the, uh, moon."

"Yes, ma'am." He looked up from Goldie's chart to survey his waiting room. "Are these all mine?"

"Nope." Sue pulled Taylor's appointment book in front of her. "Only three of them are yours."

"Is Taylor with a patient?"

"Not here yet."

Gordon searched Sue's expression. "Did she know she had morning appointments?"

"Only two of them were in the book." Sue released a ragged sigh. "Most are drop-ins."

"Hmm. I thought only vets and hairdressers had that problem." Gordon tucked Goldie's chart under his arm and stepped into the waiting room. "Sally and Goldie, are you ready to get rid of some stitches?"

"Where's the new doctor?" Gladys Jones asked. "I've been waiting forever."

"I have no idea."

Mrs. Jones dabbed her nose delicately with a tissue. "I'm allergic to dogs, you know."

Gordon gritted his teeth as he took Sally's arm. "I'll have Sue give Dr. Bowen a call and see what's keeping her. Meanwhile, there's a bench right outside where you can wait, if you prefer."

"I'm not about to miss my turn." Mrs. Jones glowered at the other waiting patients. "*I* was here first."

"I already called her," Sue said as Gordon passed the desk. "No answer. Maybe she had car trouble."

The chances of them both having car trouble the same morning were slim. Then again, having car trouble was the norm these days. Frowning, Gordon led Sally and Goldie to an exam room. It wasn't like

Taylor to be irresponsible. If she knew she had appointments, she would've been here. Only something very serious would prevent that.

Could something have happened? Was the old house really safe? Had the furnace been checked for carbon monoxide? Could the old wiring have started a fire? No, he would've heard about a fire.

"I think Goldie is much better now," Sally said as Gordon lifted the dog onto the table. "She'd sure like to get at those stitches, though."

"They itch as they heal. That's normal." Gordon exposed the neat suture line. "Taylor did a good job." *Where is she?* "Goldie's healing nicely. No sign of infection either."

"Good." Sally beamed, stroking the dog's golden fur. "I don't know what I'd do without her. There's a waiting list, and besides that, another dog just wouldn't be . . . Goldie."

Gordon cleared his throat, grateful that the dog's injury hadn't been more serious. "Well, I think she'll be with you a good long while yet. She's healthy and well cared for."

"Only the best for Goldie."

Gordon removed the stitches, then the cone around Goldie's neck. She immediately started licking the wound. Smiling, he scratched her behind the ears. "Good as new, girl, as soon as the hair grows back."

"Thank you, Doctor," Sally said with a smile.

Gordon led Sally and Goldie to the front door of the clinic and stood staring up at the rapidly darkening sky. Where was Taylor? Lightning flashed and thunder rumbled. "Do you have a ride, Sally?"

"Tom's waiting in the car. Thank you again, and please thank Dr. Bowen for me, too."

"I will." *If she ever shows up.* He watched Goldie lead Sally directly to Tom Bradshaw's blue Explorer. "That's one helluva dog you've got there, Sally."

"I know," she said without turning.

Several patients griped about Taylor's tardiness as he made his way back through the crowded waiting room. He stopped at Sue's desk and picked up Precious's chart. "Call Taylor's house again, please."

"Will do."

"Okay, Precious and Mrs. Johnson, you're next."

"Oh, Doctor, Precious is depressed," Mrs. Johnson said as she shuffled through the door Gordon held open for her.

The woman's perfume made his eyes burn, and she wore enough makeup on her wrinkled face to supply all the women in Digby.

"Do they make Prozac for Persians?" she asked without stopping.

Sue cleared her throat and Gordon rolled his eyes heavenward. Yes, his day was definitely off to a great beginning. Not.

After pronouncing Precious's diet a success and her depression a temporary stage in her adjustment to a healthier lifestyle, Gordon escorted them back to the waiting room, which was even more crowded than before.

"This is nuts." He looked at Sue. "Did you call her again?"

"Still no answer."

"Maybe someone should go check on her." He arched a brow. "Do you mind?"

Sue chewed her lower lip. "I think I should stay here to keep the peace." The phone rang and she deftly handled another disaster. "You're a real wimp and a pushover," she said as she returned the phone to its cradle. "You have one more patient; then you can run over and check on her."

Gordon narrowed his gaze, wondering if Sue was trying to play matchmaker again. Yet her suggestion made perfect sense. He had one patient and Taylor had a roomful. And Sue was definitely more adept than he at organizing chaos.

"Okay, fine." He gave the Smiths' cocker her shots and a checkup, then sent them on their way. He stopped at Sue's desk. "No Taylor yet?"

"Nope."

Gordon stripped off his lab coat. "Go ahead and start rescheduling her patients for this afternoon. I'll be right back."

He climbed into his Jeep, but it wouldn't start. Lightning split the sky again, so he immediately ruled out walking as an option. He hurried back inside and borrowed Sue's car keys, then peeled out of the parking lot in her old red Chevy. The uphol-stery was torn and there was no radio. When he'd advised her to buy something with four-wheel drive, she told him having a home for Ryan was more im-portant than a fancy car. Sue earned every dime Gordon paid her and then some, but it was still hard for her to make ends meet.

Besides, as Sue had pointed out, he had a lot of nerve advising anyone to buy a better car. Hell, at least her old Chevy ran.

As he turned the corner onto Aspen Drive, he saw Taylor's Bug at the side of the road. Making a mental note to give Sue a raise, he pulled the parking brake and killed the ignition.

He found Taylor at the rear of the car, where she was bent over, staring at something. Of course, VWs had the engine in the rear.

"I guess we *can* both have car trouble on the same day."

Taylor looked up and shook her head. "I'm sorry. I know I have patients waiting. I was getting ready to hoof it to the clinic."

"Let me have a look." Gordon shrugged. "Foreign car."

Taylor sighed. "So? Lots of people drive foreign cars these days."

"I know, but I don't understand them as well." They stood shoulder to shoulder, and he grew increasingly aware of her scent, her warmth, her nearness. "Did you check your gas gauge?"

"I stopped last night after . . ." Her cheeks flamed as he met her gaze, but she didn't look away. "I got gas on my way home last night."

The sky opened and icy sheets of rain soaked them within seconds. "Get in and try the engine," he shouted.

"You'll get wet."

"Too late." He grinned, shivering against the downpour. "Try the engine."

Taylor climbed into the car and turned the key. He heard the motor turn over, but that was it. After a few moments, she gave up and climbed out with her medical bag and purse.

"Forget it," she shouted over the rain and thunder. "I was right about giving up."

He dropped the hood and they bolted for Sue's car, both gasping as they slid across the vinyl seat. Mopping rain from his forehead, he started the engine. "N-nothing c-colder than s-summer rain at n-nine thousand f-feet."

"N-no k-kidding."

He glanced at her, sitting there dripping and shivering; then his breath left his lungs in a sudden gush. Her soaked yellow knit dress clung like a second skin, and her nipples were clearly defined beneath the wet fabric.

She turned toward him and he jerked his gaze from her tempting breasts to her face, realizing immediately that she knew exactly where he'd been looking. "I, uh . . ."

"We'd better go straight to the clinic," she said.

"No, you're soaked and Sue already rescheduled your appointments."

"Oh, then let's go to my house so I can change and you can get dry," she whispered, pushing her damp hair away from her face. "And call Sue."

He swallowed the lump in his throat, struggling against the scorching need to tug her against him, to stroke her rain-slick shoulder, to lap the sparkling droplets from her face and neck and—

*Whoa.*

No longer the least bit cold, he faced forward and turned on the windshield wipers. The windows were completely fogged over. Chuckling, he flipped the defroster to high and glanced at Taylor. Her cheeks reddened.

"Seems we're always fogging up windows," he said quietly, no longer laughing.

She turned to stare out the window as he maneuvered the Chevy away from Taylor's dead car, then down the hill to her driveway.

Taylor opened the door. "Thanks for rescuing me."

He pulled the key from the ignition and pivoted to stare at the perplexing woman again. "You're driving me crazy."

She pushed the door open farther. "Don't, Gordon." She bit her lower lip and looked away again.

Sighing, he watched her jump from the car and make a mad dash for the front door. What the hell was he going to do about this? He wanted her. He burned with the need to touch her, to taste her, to hold her. All he thought about was Taylor Bowen—what they'd had.

What they'd lost.

Angrily, he jerked open the car door and followed Taylor into the small living room, or parlor, or whatever they called rooms these days in houses built before the turn of the century. Frustration knotted in his gut as he stood dripping on a small rug in the entry.

"I'll get you a towel." Taylor disappeared through the kitchen, returning a moment later with two pink towels. "There's the phone. Call Sue while I change."

Sighing, he slipped off his shoes and dried his face and neck, then made his way to the phone. Sue picked up on the first ring. Her tone and the background racket told Gordon that things had gone from bad to worse since his departure.

"Taylor's car broke down," he said. "There's a bonus in this for you, Sue. I'm sorry for leaving you with that madhouse."

"No problem," she said in a suspiciously sweet tone. "Take as long as you need. I already rescheduled all your appointments, too. Have lunch."

*Have lunch?* This wasn't the Sue Wheeler he knew and feared. "Okay, sure." He glanced at his watch. "We'll be back by one o'clock."

"Taylor's next appointment isn't until two."

A dog barked in the background and someone sneezed. "Are you sure, Sue?"

"Positive. I have everything under control." She gave a nervous laugh. "Don't I always come through?"

Gordon hesitated. "Yeah, actually." He cleared his throat. "All right, we'll see you at two, but page me if anything comes up. Maybe one of these days we'll get a microwave tower up here so cell phones will actually work."

"Don't hold your breath." Sue laughed again; then the steady hum of a dial tone replaced his receptionist's voice in his ear.

"Okay." He hung up the phone and rubbed the towel over his head again, squeezing water out of his ponytail. Maybe he had time to run home and change, too. No, he didn't want to leave Sue there alone any longer than necessary.

"Everything all right?" Taylor asked from the bottom of the stairs.

He spun around to face her, the pink towel still clutched in his fist. She'd replaced the yellow knit dress with a blue cardigan sweater and a pair of softly faded jeans. A brand-new pair of hiking boots encased her feet.

"I see you surrendered." He flashed her a grin.

"Yep, no more sandals or sun dresses for me until I'm back down below a mile high."

The reminder that she planned to leave sliced through him, but he forcibly shoved his discomfort aside. "Do you suppose I could toss my jeans and shirt in your dryer?" He shrugged and managed a smile.

"Sure, but shouldn't we get back?" She waved her hand, indicating that he should follow. "I take it Sue was able to reschedule our appointments?"

"Super Receptionist strikes again." He tried not to watch the way Taylor's jeans hugged the cheeks of her bottom. *Perfection.*

"What time do we have to be back?" she asked over her shoulder as she led him through the kitchen.

"Uh, two."

"That late?" She pushed open a dark green swinging door. "Utility room. Help yourself."

"Sue said she'd schedule everybody after lunch. It's bound to be a late night." He stepped into the narrow doorway and looked down at his hostess.

Her green eyes sparkled as thunder rumbled in the distance. Lightning struck somewhere nearby, making the floor vibrate beneath their feet.

She was so close. So accessible. He braced himself against the wall with one arm and dropped his towel to the floor. Gently, he brushed the backs of his fingers along her cheek. She closed her eyes and leaned into the caress, igniting an inferno in his veins.

He cupped her chin in his hand and tilted her face upward. Her eyes fluttered open, their expression mirroring his conflict as if she had a direct connection to his brain. And heart.

"Don't," she whispered, her lower lip trembling. "Please."

Her words had the same effect as a frigid mountain stream. He clenched his fists and dropped his hands to his sides. "I'm sorry."

She shifted into the kitchen, deftly putting some distance between them. "I'd better call someone about my car while you're getting dry. I could heat some soup."

He cleared his throat. "Soup sounds good. Thanks." He went into the utility room and closed the door, then emptied his pockets onto the top of the dryer. He set the dryer to run on high, then leaned against the washing machine and waited. His jeans were only damp, so they shouldn't take too long.

Sue had said he should talk to Taylor. This was the perfect opportunity. They were alone. They had a couple of hours to kill. And he was in his underwear with Taylor on the other side of the door.

"Shit, don't go there."

He reeled in his wayward thoughts to Sue's lecture. Rubbing the back of his neck, he pondered his options. If he told Taylor everything, she'd realize the mistake she'd made ten years ago. Would it make any difference now?

He remembered the day he'd gone to her house and learned she was gone. Her mother had refused to speak to him, but Taylor's father hadn't hesitated. He'd told Gordon that his little girl was too good for a two-timing bastard, and that was that.

Gordon's throat had burned with unshed tears. Boys didn't cry, and he was almost a man by then.

A man with a broken heart.

Taylor had hurt him in the worst possible way. She hadn't loved him as much as he'd loved her. If she had, she would've come to him and asked for the truth. Instead, she ran away and tossed their love aside like an old pair of socks.

She hadn't come to him then for the truth. Why should he offer it to her now? It obviously wasn't important to her. No, he wouldn't volunteer anything. If Sue wanted to, that was her business. As far as he was concerned, Taylor was the one who owed him an explanation. It all boiled down to one thing.

A matter of trust.

The moment the utility room door closed, Taylor leaned against the kitchen table and counted to ten. Gordon had almost kissed her again. Even worse, she'd wanted him to.

"You cannot do this," she muttered. Gordon had

cheated on her with her best friend. How could she still want him now?

She didn't. All this was a simple case of hormones. She could handle this.

"Prove it." Gnashing her teeth, she grabbed the phone directory and opened it to *auto repair*. She had two choices in Digby. One name looked familiar, so she dialed that one. She explained her situation, then gave the man her name and address.

"I'd heard you were back in Digby," the man said. "I'll bet you don't remember me."

She glanced at the mechanic's name again. "Well, your name is familiar, but I—"

"I'm crushed," he said, chuckling. "Your brother and me played baseball together in high school."

Of course. Her brother Mike had been Digby High's starting pitcher, and Rick Miller the catcher. "Rick, yes, I do remember you."

After several minutes of small talk, Taylor arranged to have her car towed to Rick's garage, then opened a can of vegetable soup and dumped it into a pan. She grabbed some garlic bread from the freezer and turned on the oven to preheat, then stirred the soup.

Gordon was obviously going to hide in there with his clothes. *Well, fine.* He was being childish. And why hadn't he offered her an explanation about what happened between him and Sue on graduation night?

Ryan looked just like his mother, so there were no clues there. Maybe Taylor should just ask for the truth. No, if she asked, Gordon might think she cared.

She didn't, of course.

Well, not much, anyway. All right, even if Gordon wasn't Ryan's father, the fact remained that he'd slept with her best friend right after being with her. *Damn.* Taylor practically threw the bread into the oven, then glowered at the closed utility room door. What the hell was he doing in there?

Of course, he was practically naked. "Get a grip." She drew a deep breath and set the table. From now on, she would not react to Gordon or do anything to encourage his advances. Nothing.

*I'll tell him about Jeremy.*

The utility room door squeaked open and Gordon padded out carrying his socks. "All dry," he said, his tone and expression stoic. "Thanks."

"Lunch is almost ready." She poured the soup into bowls.

"Can I help?"

"Sure. There's a pitcher of tea in the fridge." She watched him put ice in the glasses, then fill them with tea. "I guess you've learned to do things for yourself, being a bachelor."

"Yep."

Why wouldn't he tell her what she wanted to know? *No, I don't care.* She grabbed a basket and retrieved the bread, then slid it across the table and took her seat across from Gordon. She really didn't care about Gordon's life.

*Liar.*

She watched his long, lean fingers grip his spoon. Those fingers had felt so gentle against her cheek. Her own hand followed her thoughts; then she reached for her napkin and placed it in her lap. She wasn't even hungry now.

"So . . . you never married?" Why had she asked him that? Small talk. That was all. Nothing more. At least she hadn't asked him about Sue.

"Nope." He spooned soup into his mouth and broke apart a piece of bread. "Thanks for lunch."

"You're welcome."

Taylor ate her soup in silence, peeved that he hadn't offered any additional information. Finally, she set her spoon aside and reached for a piece of bread. The salty, crunchy, yeasty flavor filled her mouth, and she concentrated on chewing and savoring it, forbidding that other subject from interfering with her thoughts.

"Did *you*?" he asked, startling her.

"Did I what?"

"Ever get married?"

Okay, that was a fair question. "No, school kept me too busy." *Tell him about Jeremy.*

"I remember those days myself." He took another spoonful of soup, then stared at her for several moments. "I can't believe there weren't other med students beating down your door, though."

"Well, thanks, actually—" The phone rang and she leapt up to answer it. Just when she'd found the courage to tell him about Jeremy, too.

"Hello?"

"Taylor, Rick Miller here."

"You're quick," she said, amazed to hear from him so soon.

"I went over and looked at your Bug."

"How bad is it?" She leaned against the counter, acutely aware of Gordon's rapt attention. "Is it terminal?"

Rick laughed into the phone, then said, "Nothing a tank of unleaded won't solve."

"But . . ." Taylor replayed her actions of last night. She'd stopped for five dollars' worth of gas, then bought a huge chocolate bar when she paid for the gas. She remembered killing the better part of a ten. "I got gas last night. Is there a leak somewhere?"

"I checked your fuel lines. No leaks."

"You're sure?"

"Positive, but I'll hook her up to the computer this afternoon and run her through her paces, just to be sure."

"Sure, thanks." Taylor made arrangements to stop for her car in the morning, then hung up the phone and faced Gordon. "That's so weird."

"Somebody siphon your tank?"

"In Digby?" She laughed nervously and returned to the table and took a drink of tea. "I only bought five dollars' worth, but that should've lasted me a week in this town."

He nodded and took a sip of tea. "Either there's a fuel leak, or somebody swiped it."

"That's what Rick said, too."

Gordon glanced at his watch. "I think it's time we headed back to the salt mine."

"All right." Taylor rinsed the dishes and left them in the sink, then collected her medical bag and purse from the hall closet. "I'm ready."

# THE PUBLISHERS OF ZEBRA BOUQUET

are making this special offer to lovers of contemporary romances to introduce this exciting new line of novels. Zebra's Bouquet Romances have been praised by critics and authors alike as being of the highest quality and best written romantic fiction available today.

♥

# EACH FULL-LENGTH NOVEL

has been written by authors you know and love as well as by up and coming writers that you'll only find with Zebra Bouquet. We'll bring you the newest novels by world famous authors like Vanessa Grant, Judy Gill, Ann Josephson and award winning Suzanne Barrett and Leigh Greenwood—to name just a few. Zebra Bouquet's editors have selected only the very best and highest quality for publication under the Bouquet banner.

♥

# YOU'LL BE TREATED

to glamorous settings from Carnavale in Rio, the moneyed high-powered offices of New York's Wall Street, the rugged north coast of British Columbia, and the mountains of North Carolina. Bouquet Romances use these settings to spin tales of star-crossed lovers that are sure to captivate you. These stories will keep you enthralled to the very happy end.

♥

# 4 FREE NOVELS
As a way to introduce you to these terrific romances, the publishers of Bouquet are offering Zebra Romance readers Four Free Bouquet novels. They are yours for the asking with no obligation to buy a single book. Read them at your leisure. We are sure that after you've read these introductory books you'll want more! (If you do not wish to receive any further Bouquet novels, simply write "cancel" on the invoice and return to us within 10 days.)

# SAVE 20% WITH HOME DELIVERY
Each month you'll receive four just published Bouquet Romances. We'll ship them to you as soon as they are printed (you may even get them before the bookstores). You'll have 10 days to preview these exciting novels for Free. If you decide to keep them, you'll be billed the special preferred home subscription price of just $3.20 per book; a total of just $12.80 — that's a savings of 20% off the publisher's price. If for any reason you are not satisfied simply return the novels for full credit, no questions asked. You'll never have to purchase a minimum number of books and you may cancel your subscription at any time.

## GET STARTED TODAY –
## NO RISK AND NO OBLIGATION

To get your introductory gift of 4 Free Bouquet Romances fill out and mail the enclosed Free Book Certificate today. We'll ship your free selections as soon as we receive this information. Remember that you are under no obligation. This is a risk free offer from the publishers of
Zebra Bouquet Romances.

# FREE BOOK CERTIFICATE

Yes! I would like to take you up on your offer. Please send me 4 Free Bouquet Romance Novels as my introductory gift. I understand that unless I tell you otherwise, I will then receive the 4 newest Bouquet novels to preview each month Free for 10 days. If I decide to keep them I'll pay the preferred home subscriber's price of just $3.20 each (a total of only $12.80) plus $1.50 for shipping and handling. That's a 20% savings off the publisher's price. I understand that I may return any shipment for full credit no questions asked and I may cancel this subscription at any time with no obligation. Regardless of what I decide to do, the 4 Free introductory novels are mine to keep as Bouquet's gift.

Name _____

Address _____ Apt. _____

City _____ State _____ Zip _____

Telephone ( ____ ) _____

Signature _____ BN010A

(If under 18, parent or guardian must sign.)

For your convenience you may charge your shipments automatically to a Visa or MasterCard so you'll never have to worry about late payments and missing shipments. If you return any shipment we'll credit your account.
Yes, charge my credit card for my "Bouquet Romance" shipments until I tell you otherwise.
☐ Visa ☐ MasterCard

Account Number _____

Expiration Date _____

Signature _____

Orders subject to acceptance by Zebra Home Subscription Service. Terms and Prices subject to change.
Offer valid in U.S. only.

BOUQUET ROMANCE

120 Brighton Road
P.O. BOX 5214
Clifton, New Jersey 07015-5214

Gordon held the door open for her; then Taylor made sure it locked behind them. If someone would steal gas from her car, then Digby wasn't the same safe little town she remembered.

"At least the rain stopped." He paused on the front lawn and stood there with his hands shoved into his pockets.

The sight of him standing in front of the same house where she'd grown up, staring off at the horizon, reopened all her wounds. She couldn't take her eyes off him as he spread his arms out to his sides and drew a deep breath.

"It smells so good." He flashed her a crooked grin, his turquoise eyes twinkling.

Sunlight broke through the clouds and a rainbow appeared behind Gordon, framing him. What woman wouldn't stare at a man who looked like the pot of gold at the end of the rainbow?

All the times she'd waited for him on this porch flooded her mind. Nothing in her youth had meant as much to her as seeing Gordon Lane.

Nothing.

And nothing had ever hurt as much as losing him.

# EIGHT

Gordon holed up in his office most of the afternoon, seeing only two more patients and calling the University of Northern Colorado about Patches. Unfortunately, the UNC lab hadn't found anything either. The mutt had to be allergic to something, but what?

Deciding to go through the dog's entire chart one more time before giving Sue the lab results, he leaned back and stared at his copious notes. The words blurred and ran together, and Taylor's face took their place in his mind's eye.

*Damn.* Why couldn't he stop thinking about her? Maybe Sue was right. After all these years, he should be able to confront Taylor about her abandonment and the truth. They were both adults now. Professionals. Mature. Reasonable.

Well, where Taylor was concerned, he was far from reasonable. With a sigh, he dropped the chart to his desk and rubbed the back of his aching neck. He could've left hours ago—assuming his Jeep would start—but he hadn't.

And he knew why he was still here. "Go ahead

and deny it, Lane," he muttered, knowing it was past time to put this mess to rest. The only way to deal with this was to face it. He still had feelings for Taylor. Strong feelings. And he suspected that she still cared about him, too.

Remembering the way she'd felt in his arms last night in front of City Hall ignited his blood. She'd responded to his kiss enthusiastically. She wanted him, and he sure as hell wanted her, but it was more than that. Much more.

Lust was simple.

Love was a real pain.

*Yes, love.* Had the past poisoned them both too much to go back? Could there ever be anything between them again? The thought warmed him, and he drew a long, slow breath. He wanted this.

He wanted Taylor.

And not just sexually, either. He wanted her in his life as a friend, a confidante, and—he hoped—a lover. His body sprang to life at this thought, reminding him of how far he'd backslid on self-control since Taylor's return. He felt like a teen again. Next thing he knew, his face would break out and his hair would *un*gray. He rubbed his chin. Hell, maybe he could give up shaving, too.

"I've got it bad." At least he'd faced it. He stood and poured himself a cup of coffee, then went to stare out the window. The sun had shone all afternoon following this morning's storm—a perfect summer day in the Rockies.

Yes, he would talk to Taylor this evening. He'd face the ghosts of their past, tell her why Sue had believed what she'd told Taylor to be true. Then he'd wait for her to explain why she ran away without at least talking to him. If she had, things would've been so different.

He knew without a doubt that they would be married by now, and maybe they'd be starting a family. The thought of Taylor bearing his child made his chest ache with longing. He'd denied this long enough. Yes, Sue was right. He was still crazy about Taylor Bowen.

Suddenly eager to carry out his plans, he set the cup on his desk and opened the door. He'd been hiding from everything far too long. With a spring in his step, he made his way to the reception desk, smiling when he found the waiting room empty.

"Wow, that's different." He flashed Sue a grin. "Thanks for handling everything today."

"It's my job." She narrowed her eyes and gave him a suspicious look. "What's up, Doc?"

"I've been doing some serious thinking." He clasped his hands behind his back and rocked back on his heels.

"And . . . ?"

"I can't tell you." He bent down and kissed her on the cheek. "Is Taylor still here?"

Sue smiled and released a long, slow breath. "Does this mean you've decided to be reasonable about . . ."

"Maybe." Gordon shrugged. "Is she still here?"

"Yes, with her last patient." She bit her lower lip. "Gordon, I'm so pleased about this."

"No more Ms. Hyde?"

She shook her head, and a tear slipped from the corner of her eye. "Sheesh, look what you made me do." Laughing, she mopped the tear away with a tissue. "I want a full report."

"Some things a man doesn't even share with his receptionist," he teased, hoping there would be really something to share. "Besides, we don't know that this will change things at all."

"I'm sure everything will—"

"No, don't jinx it."

Sue laughed again. "Since when are you superstitious?"

"Just being cautious. I gave Hank the night off, since we don't have any overnight patients. I have some paperwork to finish up." He turned to leave the reception area. "Oh, before I forget, the report from UNC on Patches didn't show anything at all. We're still at square one."

"It has to be an allergy." Sue shook her head. "But to what?"

"That's what I said. Start a diary of his diet; then we'll start examining his surroundings. Again."

"I guess there's nothing else we can do."

"Tell Ryan no table scraps, and would you mind letting Taylor know I need to see her before she leaves?"

"Mind? My pleasure." Sue reached for the ringing phone. "Digby Veterinary Clinic." She rolled her eyes at Gordon. "Yes, it's also the Digby Medical Clinic. For now."

He headed back to his office, feeling hopeful and truly happy for the first time since Taylor's return.

Of course, she could make him crash and burn by refusing to give them a second chance, but at least then he'd know.

"I'll give her the message," Sue said into the phone.

The tone of her voice prompted Gordon to pause, and he turned around to watch Sue pick up the message she'd just taken. She read a fax number back to the caller, then said she'd remind Taylor to send written directions to find Digby from Denver.

Was her brother coming to visit at last? He hadn't seen Mike Bowen since graduation. But why would Mike need directions? Curious about when he was coming, Gordon lingered until Sue hung up the phone.

"Was that Mike?" he asked.

Sue gasped. "I thought you went back to your office. You darn near gave me a heart attack."

"Sorry." He gestured toward the message. "Is Mike coming to visit?"

"No, the message was from someone else." She shoved the slip of paper to the side of her desk and pulled Gordon's appointment book in front of her. "You have a nine o'clock tomorrow." She arched a brow. "Is your Jeep going to make it?"

"I don't even know if it'll make it home tonight." Had Sue deliberately changed the subject? "Nine. I'll be here. I can ride my bike if the weather cooperates."

"All right, go finish your work so you'll be free to talk to Taylor when she's finished."

"Slave driver." Gordon winked and headed toward his office. He must've been imagining things. Whatever the message was that Sue had taken, it couldn't compete with his plans for this evening. Tonight, he would plot a course for the future.

With Taylor. He hoped.


Sue buried her face in her hands and groaned the moment Gordon was out of earshot. Who the hell was Dr. Jeremy Cole, and why was he coming to see Taylor? Of course, it stood to reason that Taylor had a boyfriend. She was young and attractive, after all.

"I have to *do* something." She looked at the message again and a smile tugged at the corners of her mouth. Dr. Cole would need a tour guide. Sue leafed through Taylor's appointment book. And Dr. Bowen had a very full schedule. Or at least she would, once Sue was finished with it.

She wrote out rather creative directions to Digby from Denver, then fed the paper through the fax machine to Dr. Cole. He'd still get here, but it would take him a while.

After the fax went through successfully, she leaned back in her chair with a contented sigh. She needed to plan Dr. Cole's itinerary now. After all, showing Taylor's visitor around Digby and making sure he didn't get bored was the least she could do to help.

The very least.


Taylor wrote an antibiotic prescription for her last—she hoped it was her last—patient of the day, and showed the woman to the door. "Make sure you take the entire prescription, Mrs. Odin."

"I will."

Taylor leaned against the doorjamb and met Sue's gaze. "Are we finished now? Can I just drop right here and go to sleep?"

Sue laughed and handed Taylor a stack of messages, then headed toward the front door with a ring of keys. She sent the lock home, then turned off the lights in the waiting room and drew the shades across the entire front of the building. "That's it. Only emergencies can find you now."

Taylor smiled as memories flooded her. She and Sue had once been so close. They'd laughed and cried together from kindergarten through high school. Remembering that their high school graduation had signaled the end of everything, Taylor cringed inwardly. She couldn't blame Sue exclusively for that, though. Gordon was far from innocent.

Retreating into her emotional safe, Taylor looked over her messages. Pharmaceutical sales reps had found her. Somehow, she'd thought she might dodge that bullet in Digby, but patients appreciated free samples, and she would need supplies.

The message at the bottom of her stack gave her pause. "Oh, nuts, I forgot about Jeremy."

"Taylor, good, you're still here."

Gordon's voice startled her and she dropped the messages. They both bent to retrieve them, and his warm hand brushed against hers, sending a shiver up her arm and straight to her core.

He handed her the messages as they straightened.

The intensity of his turquoise eyes singed her. Something was different. More compelling. She held her breath, drowning in a tidal wave of memory-flavored sensation.

Last night's kiss, the feel of him pressed against her, his lips on hers, his hands . . . Liquid fire washed through her and she swayed, suddenly dizzy with intoxicating images from the past.

"Well, I'm outta here," Sue announced, heading down the hall at her typical overdrive speed. "I already faxed Dr. Cole directions to Digby for you."

"Oh, thanks." Taylor stared after Sue, her brow furrowed. She looked at the message again, noticing Sue's scribbled note at the bottom this time: *Faxed driving directions to Jeremy Cole, M.D., 17:40 today.*

The back door slammed and Sue was gone. Only the light in the reception area remained on, bathing Gordon in gold and silver. Though the summer days were long, once the sun dipped behind the highest peak, Digby fell into the shadows. The sky above could remain semiblue for an hour or more after lights were required by earthbound mortals.

"I'm glad you're still here, Taylor," Gordon said, facing her. "There's something I want to talk to you about. I think it's time to put the past behind us."

It was *definitely* time to tell him about Jeremy.

She swallowed hard and licked her lips. "It was nice of Sue to send that fax for me. Jeremy is a friend from med school." Of course, *friend* wasn't quite the right word. "He's coming to visit."

"That's nice."

She met Gordon's gaze, his expression more sol-

emn than before. Now was the time. He'd know
soon enough that Jeremy was more than just a friend
to Taylor. "He's my—"

"Oh, no, I just realized something." Gordon rolled
his eyes toward the ceiling and chuckled. "If the Jeep
won't start, we're both stuck here without wheels."

"We've been so busy this afternoon, I didn't have
time to call Rick about my car." Her heart pressed
against her throat as she tried to summon the courage to tell Gordon everything about Jeremy. Her car
was really the last thing on her mind. In fair weather
she could walk home, so its absence wasn't a major
crisis now.

Standing here alone with Gordon *was.*

"Taylor, I . . ."

A flicker in the aqua depths of his eyes awakened
something warm and vibrant from deep within her.
Something she'd tried to keep safe. Protected.

Frozen.

But now her chest filled with a sweet ache and his
heat bore into her even from the foot or so that separated them. Drunk from his nearness, she inhaled
his essence, basked in the intensity of his perusal.

She wanted him.

A tremor skittered down her spine and she
wrapped her arms around her abdomen, as if to protect her heart and soul from the delicious agony of
wanting Gordon Lane again, and remembering all
the reasons she couldn't have him. And *shouldn't*
want him.

He reached out to brush his fingers against her
cheek. He'd often done that when they were dating,

touching her as if he feared she might break. The boy she'd loved more than anything was still in there, lurking behind the tiny lines at the corners of his eyes and the silver hair. Was the Gordon Lane who'd betrayed her still there as well?

Her throat constricted and she held her breath as he took a step closer, his breath fanning her cheek and her torment. "Gordon . . ."

"Shh, don't talk." He drew a deep breath and continued to caress her face with the tips of his fingers. "I have a lot of things to tell you, Taylor."

Her heart slammed against her ribs and a soft roar commenced in her head. "I . . . but . . ."

"It's time to face the past"—he cupped her cheek in his palm and came closer—"and the future."

*The future?* She drew a sharp breath. What was he saying? Surely not—

"Last night proved something to me," he continued, framing her face with both hands now, stroking her eyebrows and temples with his thumbs. "We still have feelings for each other, Taylor. Powerful feelings."

How could she argue that point? She tried to speak, but words failed her. In his arms last night, she'd felt alive and on fire for the first time since leaving Digby. And Gordon. When he kissed her, touched her, looked at her, she felt worshiped. Desired.

Loved.

*Loved?* He lowered his mouth to hers, nibbling at her lower lip until she sought his mouth herself and fully connected. He crushed her against him, delving into her mouth with his tongue as if seeking buried treasure. She moaned and leaned into him, taking and giving with all she had.

Something snapped inside her, and all the hunger and need she'd suppressed surged forth, took command, banished common sense, not to mention any thoughts of Jeremy. *Jeremy who?* Drowning, she clung to him, seeking more and more of what he had to offer. She wanted it all.

And she wanted it now.

With trembling fingers, she reached between them and tugged his shirt from the waistband of his jeans, deftly releasing the buttons until his hard, bare chest was exposed. Moaning, she pressed the flat of her palm against him. He growled into their kiss and pushed her lab coat off her shoulders, letting it drift unheeded to the floor.

Scalding need shot through her and she clenched against that unbearable emptiness again. Gordon released the tiny buttons at the front of her sweater and shoved it aside. Cool air touched her bare midriff and her nipples hardened against her thin cotton bra.

Gasping, he broke their kiss and stared intently into her eyes. "Taylor, I . . ."

She pressed her finger to his lips. "Don't talk." If she was making a mistake, she didn't want to know it until later. Now all she wanted was Gordon. All of him. "Don't think."

Still staring into her eyes, he brought his hand to her breast, testing its weight, brushing his thumb against its rigid peak. She gasped, and he wrapped his other arm around her waist, bending her back and lifting her breasts to him in offering. *Oh, yes.*

His mouth. She wanted his mouth on her. He trailed tiny kisses along her collarbone, skimmed the lace trim that edged her bra with his teeth, then covered her nipple with his hot mouth right through the fabric.

Taylor sucked in a breath and clutched him to her. He drew her into his mouth, sending spirals of longing cascading through her. She wanted skin. His. Hers. Theirs.

He rolled her other nipple between his thumb and forefinger, making her ache and swell against the flimsy fabric. Then he unhooked the clasp at the front of her bra, releasing her swollen breasts from the confining garment. He pulled back, exposing her breasts to his gaze. Cool air found her damp nipple and she ached for his warmth again.

His expression was reverent, reminding Taylor that Gordon had always treated her this way. Like she was special and important. And beautiful.

"Perfect," he whispered, covering her nipple again with his mouth.

She moaned, staring at the startling contrast between his tanned face and her milk-white breast. He sucked gently, then hungrily, then nipped and teased her with his teeth, driving her madder with each passing second. Each tug produced an answering echo of unbearable emptiness from her womb.

She shouldn't do this. They shouldn't do this. She shouldn't even *want* this.

*Shouldn't, be damned.* Every second since the morning she'd found him in the creek had been leading to this. She stroked his bare shoulders, kneaded his back, held him against her. There was no turning back now. They would make love right here in his waiting room.

*Make love.* The thought fueled her desire like gasoline on an open flame. "Gordon, I—"

The phone rang, startling them both. Gordon jerked upright, barely saving her from falling to the floor. Laughing, he pressed his forehead against hers and reached for the phone. "I hope this isn't an emergency, because I think we have one right here that's pretty critical."

Taylor nodded, her breathing labored, her bare flesh coated with a fine film of perspiration. She wanted him so much it hurt. Yes, critical was a good word. She'd deal with the side effects later.

Still watching her, he brought the receiver to his ear and his hand back to her naked breast, gently stoking the fire he'd started. "Hello? I mean, Digby Clinic."

"Taylor? Uh, sure." A few moments of silence and Gordon's changing expression told her he was listening. "I . . . think you'd better talk to her. Just a minute." A frown creased his brow and he dropped his hand from her breast. Clearing his throat, he handed her the phone. "Jeremy Cole needs to know if he should get a hotel room or if he'll be staying with you."

*Oh.* Her hand trembled as she took the phone from Gordon. "I . . . uh . . . just a minute." She put the receiver to her ear. "Jeremy," she said, hoping her voice didn't betray her frazzled state. "When are you coming?"

"I'll be there Friday," Jeremy said. "I've missed you." His voice dropped and Taylor cringed. "Got room for a lonely doctor at your place?"

An icy chill swept over her and she glanced at Gordon's stricken expression. Without a word, he retrieved his shirt and buttoned it, then walked away. She didn't hear the back door close and figured he must have gone to his office.

"Taylor, you still there?"

"Yes, Jeremy, I'm here." She cleared her throat and searched her mind. "I don't believe it would be appropriate for you to stay at my place. Digby is a small town."

"Who cares what those old fogies think?"

"I care." Mentally counting to ten, she bent down to retrieve her bra. After a lot of contorting, she finally managed to squirm into it. "I'm the local doctor right now, and I don't intend to cause a scandal." *Unless it's with the local veterinarian.* "Besides, we haven't been . . . I mean, you and I haven't, uh . . ."

"I know, but you know I'm ready." That husky tone entered Jeremy's voice again.

"But I'm not." Her answer was abrupt and cruel, but also true. She glanced at the empty doorway, hoping Gordon hadn't left. It was time to settle things between them, one way or another.

"All right, so give me the number of the nearest hotel," Jeremy said, obviously disappointed.

"Hotel?" Taylor picked up her sweater and slipped

her arms into it, then held the phone to her ear with her shoulder while she buttoned the front. "Digby doesn't have a—no, wait." She couldn't tell him that, or he'd insist on staying with her. Desperate, she found the local phone directory in Sue's desk drawer and flipped open the pages. "Ah, here it is. There's a bed-and-breakfast in the center of town, and some guest cabins in the mountains at the edge of town. I'll call and see if there are vacancies."

"If there aren't . . . ?"

Taylor winced and wiped her sweaty palm against her jeans. "We'll worry about that *if* it's an issue."

"You know how I feel about you, Taylor."

No, actually, she didn't, and right now she didn't want to, because she felt nothing toward Jeremy but irritation. All she could think of was the stricken look on Gordon's face. "I have another call, Jeremy," she lied. "Emergency. See you Friday."

She hung up the phone and drew a deep breath, then picked her lab coat up off the floor and draped it over her arm. Slowly, she made her way down the hall to Gordon's office. He was busy looking through a chart and making some notes.

"Gordon, I—"

"Don't." He looked up at her, his expression guarded. "I should've realized a beautiful woman like you would have a boyfriend."

"He isn't my boyfriend. Exactly."

His brow arched. "Oh?"

"Well, we've dated, but . . ." She sighed. "Gordon, we need to talk."

He shook his head and leaned back in his chair

with a sigh. "I had planned to talk to you tonight, but I got a little carried away." A derisive chuckle left his lips and he twirled a pencil between his fingers. When he met her gaze again, all the warmth had vanished. "I'm sorry, Taylor. I had no right to touch you, but at least that kept me from saying things I would regret."

*Sorry?* She'd rather have been slapped. "No, please, you don't understand." She approached his desk, not sure what to say. She ached for this man physically, and her heart mourned the loss of what they'd once shared.

What they no longer shared, because of his infidelity.

She froze in midstep, pride banishing all the warmth and desire she'd known in his embrace a few moments earlier. Gordon Lane had cheated on her with her best friend. God, what was she thinking?

"I called Rick Miller," Gordon said, his tone unemotional. "He's bringing your car by."

Her eyes burned, but she lifted her chin and drew a deep breath through her nose, releasing it through her mouth. Deep breathing, relaxation, focus. That's what she needed to banish the tears, to bring her hormones and wayward emotions under control.

"Thank you." She turned and headed toward the door. "I'll wait for him out front."

She glanced over her shoulder. The pained expression in Gordon's eyes tormented her, but he quickly masked it. A few moments ago she'd been ready to forgive everything, to surrender her pride once and for all to a man who'd hurt her in the worst possible way.

*Fool.* Without another word, she headed down the hall to her office. She hung her lab coat on a hook and grabbed her medical bag and purse, then returned to the waiting room. After unlocking the door, she stepped out into the cool mountain air and relocked the door behind her.

The evening's chill penetrated her thin sweater and her heart. She mustn't let Gordon get to her again like this. Renewing her relationship with him would be stupid and futile. Besides, she couldn't trust him. He might hurt her again.

Remembering the stricken look on his face a few moments ago, understanding struck. She looked back over her shoulder at the closed door. The shade fell back into place, and she realized he'd been watching her.

Yes, she'd definitely learned something new this evening about Gordon Lane. Guilt was a new emotion for her to feel toward him. Of course, she hadn't realized it until today.

He'd hurt her more than anyone in her entire life.

And the feeling was mutual.

# NINE

After tucking Ryan and Patches into bed, Sue surrendered to the urge to call Gordon. She'd tell him she was just making sure he made it home as an excuse, but he'd know what she really wanted to hear.

He picked up on the third ring. "Hello?"

"Gordon, it's Sue."

Silence. Maybe he wasn't alone. She'd never forgive herself if she interrupted a romantic moment between Gordon and Taylor. "Uh, are you alone?"

Something resembling a snort came through the receiver.

"I'll take that as a yes, then," she said. *Darn it all.* "How . . . did it go with Taylor after I left?" *Gee, that's subtle.*

"I don't want to discuss Taylor."

"So we're back to that?" Sighing, Sue slid down the wall to the floor, pulling her knees up to her chest. "I thought you decided to put the past in the past where it belongs."

"Dumb idea." He cleared his throat. "A moment of weakness. Besides, she has a man in her life who's serious enough about her to come for a visit. You talked to him. Remember?"

"You mean Dr. Cole?" Sue bit her lower lip, renewing her vow to make Jeremy Cole's visit a nonissue. "We don't know he's the man in her life, and even if—"

"No. It won't work."

"But—"

"No." His tone was adamant. "Give it a rest. I'm over it. Time to move on."

*Yeah, sure, like you haven't had the last ten years to move on, buddy.* She rolled her eyes and swallowed her frustration. "I'm very sorry." *But it's far from over, Gordon Lane.*

"Yeah," he said, his voice low and gruff. "Me, too. 'Night."

She rose slowly and hung up the wall phone, then grabbed her tarot cards from the junk drawer. After lighting a red candle this time—red for passion—she plopped into a chair at her kitchen table and shuffled the oversized deck, then cut the cards, concentrating on Taylor and Gordon and what they'd once shared.

No matter what it took, she would get them together again. Gordon and Taylor belonged together. They were so much in love, and it was all her fault that they weren't together right this minute. Taylor coming back to Digby after all these years was fate, and Sue believed in fate. "Serendipity," she murmured with a sniffle.

Blinking back her tears, she whispered, "How can I get Gordon and Taylor back together?" She drew one card and turned it over on the table. "The Moon again? What is it about the moon? Couldn't you be a little more specific this time? Sheesh."

She glanced at the calendar on the wall. *What about the moon?* There would be a full one in less than two weeks. Did that mean something? Of course it did. Otherwise, she wouldn't have drawn the same card twice in answer to the same question.

Nodding, she drew a second card. "The Lovers. Hey, now we're getting somewhere." With a smug smile, she placed that card beside the Moon. All she had to do was get Taylor and Gordon together during the full moon. Right?

"Yeah, real simple." Two more stubborn people had never been born. "All right, cards, what can *I* do to help get these two together again?" She reached for a third card and placed it beside the other two. "Eight of Swords, whatever that means." She grabbed the booklet and flipped through the pages until she came to the right card.

Her gaze zeroed in on the card, showing a blindfolded woman bound with a rope and surrounded by eight swords driven into the ground. Then she looked at the card's description and explanation. One word leapt off the page and she swallowed hard, knowing what she had to do.

She'd caused this problem in the first place, and it was up to her to fix it. Only one thing would set her free and allow Gordon and Taylor to be together again. Gordon refused to do it, so Sue would have to.

She looked at the open booklet in her hand, and the word burned itself into her brain.

*Truth.*

Taylor made reservations for Jeremy at the Digby Bed-and-Breakfast, then headed out the door for the office. Today marked the beginning of her new attitude toward Gordon. She would behave in a professional manner, speak to him only when absolutely necessary, and absolutely *not* touch him. Or let him touch her . . .

She and Jeremy had an understanding, after all. Well, that wasn't entirely true. Jeremy wanted commitment from her and she hadn't given it yet. Maybe that's what she needed to do now. It would help her put the past behind her.

But the thought of accepting Jeremy's marriage proposal right now made her stomach clench and her head pound. She would have three years in Digby to make up her mind. No reason to decide right now.

Three more years near Gordon.

She paused on the front porch and locked the door, trying to ignore the pounding of her heart as she remembered the feel of Gordon's hands and mouth on her last night. "Never again," she muttered, clutching her keys in a death grip as she trotted down the steps. The only defense she had against Gordon's charm was distance.

Having Jeremy in town would help, though she was relieved that he wouldn't be staying at her place.

She wondered how she would keep him busy through a long weekend, but all thoughts fled just shy of her car.

The bear was back.

Yesterday's storm had left her dirt driveway the consistency of soup, and now the mud was hardening around dozens of huge bear prints. She unlocked her car, then opened the door and jumped inside. Looking quickly around the yard, she assured herself that there was no bear here now.

The flesh around her mouth tingled and her breathing came in short gasps. After a few minutes she swallowed her fear and buckled her seat belt. She'd call the animal control people from the office. Starting her car, she wondered if Digby even had animal control. Well, she intended to find out. There had to be some way of keeping bears in the woods where they belonged.

And far away from her.

She wiped her sweaty palms on her jeans, then dropped the car into reverse. Yes, she was being very reasonable now, despite her understandable phobia about bears. This would all be fine.

She parked her Bug beside Gordon's Jeep and hurried through the back door. Inside, she drew a deep breath and squared her shoulders. She could do this professional, aloof thing. *Sure, piece of cake.* There really was no reason for her to talk to Gordon at all beyond common courtesy, and there was *definitely* no reason for her to be alone with him again. Ever.

Girding herself for battle—against herself—she retrieved her lab coat from her office and headed for

Sue and her appointment book. Today was bound to be better than yesterday.

The waiting room was nearly empty. Taylor stared in awe. "Did you run them all off?" she asked Sue.

Chuckling, Sue pointed to Taylor's appointment book. "Only two appointments today, but most of yesterday's were walk-ins. Remember?"

"Oh, yeah." But hadn't Sue said she had a full schedule? Taylor sighed and glanced at the appointment book. "I suppose once people get used to having me in town, they'll remember to call for an appointment."

"Well, I wouldn't bet on it, but I'll post a sign and also make up a brochure about our appointment policy."

"Thanks." She gave Sue a long look. "Gordon's right—you *are* Wonder Woman."

Sue's cheeks flushed crimson and she ducked her head. "Just my job."

"Do you happen to have the number for Digby Animal Control?"

Sue frowned. "Gordon *is* Animal Control in Digby, but he's in surgery this morning."

*Figures.* "I had bear tracks in my yard again this morning."

"Bear? That far into town?" Sue's eyes widened. "Again? What do you mean *again*?"

"This is the second time at the house." Icy fingers of fear wrapped themselves around Taylor's heart. "I'm not very rational about bears. Especially stalking ones."

"I remember." Sue's tone and expression were

sympathetic. "We'll talk to Gordon about it. You don't have a hummingbird feeder up, do you?"

"No, I know better than that. Those things are pure bear bait." Taylor gave a nervous chuckle. "I grew up around here, remember?"

"Yeah, I do." Sue's voice quieted and she released a long sigh. "Gordon won't be seeing regular patients today at all, but I'll make sure to tell him about the bear if you don't get the chance."

The front door opened and Ryan dashed through it. "Hey, Mom," he said. "I forgot my lunch."

"Sure you did," Sue said, reaching for her purse. "Why didn't you say something when you were here earlier?"

Ryan lifted a bony shoulder. "Dunno."

Sue handed her son a few bills. "Go straight to Mrs. Lane's after school or she'll worry."

"I will. She's baking peanut butter cookies today with those little butterscotch things in them." Shoving the bills into his pocket, Ryan shot Taylor a curious look, then raced out the door again, sending the bells into a frenzy.

So Gordon's mother watched Ryan after school and baked him cookies. Taylor chewed her lower lip as she considered this bit of information, then remembered that none of this was supposed to matter to her anymore. *The New Deal, remember?*

"I swear, that boy never walks anywhere," Sue said with a laugh. She dropped her purse into the bottom drawer and closed it. "I wish I had that much energy."

Taylor couldn't prevent her grin. Sue had more energy than God. "You do all right."

Sue's expression sobered. "Taylor, I'd like for us to have a little talk about something. Something that's long overdue."

Liquid fire flooded Taylor's face and her mouth went dry. "There's nothing to talk about."

"Yes, there is, and you know what I mean. We both know." Sue grabbed Taylor's hand, her expression pleading. "Please? Just give me one evening out of your life to explain everything; then I'll never mention it again."

Taylor met Sue's gaze, saw the woman's anguish, and remembered all the good times they'd shared as children. Though Sue had betrayed her, Taylor couldn't find it in her heart to deny her this one chance to clear her conscience. Whatever Sue had to say wouldn't change anything, but it would at least satisfy her curiosity and give closure to the whole mess.

"All right." Taylor leaned over and flipped open the appointment book to the following weeks. "You know my schedule better than I do. Come over for dinner tonight and we'll—"

"No, that's too early."

Frowning, Taylor met Sue's frantic gaze. "Too early for what?"

"The full moon." Sue's cheeks bloomed with color again. "Never mind. Oh, look, this coming Tuesday looks good, and Ryan will be gone on an overnight field trip to Denver with his class."

"All right, Tuesday." Taylor studied the tremendous relief that crossed Sue's features. Why? "Come by about seven?"

"Great, I'll bring pizza and wine."

Sue's enthusiasm made Taylor uncomfortable. They weren't exactly friends anymore, after all. "I'll get something chocolate." Their favorite treat as teens had been brownies topped with rocky road ice cream. Besides, she had a feeling they'd both need it by then. *And* the wine.

"Thank you, Taylor." Sue squeezed her hand and smiled. "You won't be sorry. I promise."

*I already am.* Dread pressed down on Taylor. Would she be forced to relive the events that had made her leave Digby the first time? "Well, so what time is my first appointment?" The cat bells sounded again and Mrs. Johnson came through the door, sans Precious.

Sue gave Taylor a tight smile. "Now?"

"Ooookay." Taylor drew a deep breath and straightened.

"Mrs. Johnson, you're right on time," Sue said. "And I believe you already know Dr. Bowen."

"Yes, but she'd better forget all those newfangled ways they teach doctors nowadays," Mrs. Johnson muttered, giving Taylor the evil eye. "I want good, old-fashioned medical care, like Dr. Hardy—God rest his soul—from *General Hospital.*"

"We aim to please, Mrs. Johnson," Taylor said, trying not to grin. She headed down the hall with the elderly woman at her side. "What seems to be the problem?"

"Well, lan' sakes." Mrs. Johnson gave her a look

of utter disbelief. "If I knew that, I certainly wouldn't need you."

"Uh, well, then what are your symptoms?" Taylor held the door open to the exam room. "Why don't we start with those?"

Mrs. Johnson turned to face Taylor and held her hand over her heart and leaned closer. "Close the door, please." She took several deep breaths. "You promise not to tell a soul?"

*Oh, that's an absolute guarantee.* "Of course. The doctor-patient relationship is completely confidential, Mrs. Johnson." Taylor closed the door behind them and gripped the woman's elbow to guide her to the examination table. "Now what seems to be the trouble?"

"Well," Mrs. Johnson said in a low voice, "I used the public rest room at Gertie's Diner, and I never do that as a rule, but just this once I couldn't wait."

Taylor cleared her throat and checked Mrs. Johnson's pulse while she waited. When her patient didn't volunteer any additional information, she asked, "Is there a problem with the rest room at Gertie's Diner?"

The woman gasped and appeared scandalized. "Oh, dear, but I'm afraid there is." She held her hand over her abdomen. "Gertie only has one rest room"—she leaned very close—"for men *and* women to share."

"Okay." Taylor waited for the punch line.

"Dear me." Mrs. Johnson waved her hand in front of her face like a fan. "That young mechanic, Kent Donahue, from Miller's Garage went in there first."

Taylor didn't say a word, but her eyes widened slightly. "I'm listening, Mrs. Johnson."

The older woman cupped a hand to her mouth. "I've missed my monthly curse."

Taylor coughed into her hand to prevent her shock from showing. She hoped. "Oh, I see, and you believe that's related somehow to the rest room at Gertie's Diner?"

"Well, Kent was in there a long time." She lifted her chin a notch. "Like father, like son, if you ask me."

Taylor made some notes on the chart that had nothing to do with the Donahue men. "Well, I think we should start with your medical history; then maybe we'll order some tests." *Unless I can convince the woman this is impossible.*

Mrs. Johnson gasped. "Oh, dear. I was afraid of that. This very thing happened to poor Martha on *The Daring and the Dauntless.*"

Taylor's lips twitched, but she maintained her stoicism with great effort. "So, tell me, Mrs. Johnson," she continued, summoning her most solemn expression, "what *was* the date of your last menstrual period—er, I mean monthly curse?" She batted her lashes furiously, hoping she appeared more innocent than she felt. A crash course on the life expectancy of sperm on toilet seats was probably out of the question, not to mention the fact that Mrs. Johnson probably hadn't ovulated in a quarter century or so.

"Old Doc Eddington never would have used a word like"—she leaned closer still—"*that* around a lady." Despite her chastisement, Mrs. Johnson seemed satisfied that Taylor took her plight seriously. She looked down at her stubby legs swinging to and fro as they dangled off the exam table. "I remember it clearly. It was the year after my dear Harold passed away."

"And that was when?" Taylor waited, pen poised in midair, trying to remember a time when Mrs. Johnson had been married. Even during Taylor's childhood, Mrs. Johnson had been an eccentric widow with about a hundred cats in residence.

"July 22, 1970."

Gordon spayed the Wilsons' cat, neutered the Smiths' dog, and completed brilliant reconstructive hip surgery on Sheriff Nankeville's aging collie before lunch. Standing at his sink lathering soap to his elbows, he clenched his teeth and tried not to think about Taylor. Or last night. Or his life in general.

Once upon a time he'd planned to teach the same surgical technique he'd just used on the collie to veterinary students. His father's death had brought him back to Digby, where he'd fallen into the old man's practice and never managed to escape again.

The brutal truth was, Digby didn't need a full-time veterinarian. Sighing, Gordon nudged the water faucet off with his elbow and grabbed a paper towel. He enjoyed his practice, but it just wasn't enough. More and more, he found himself fantasizing about life beyond Digby. Maybe in Denver. Or at the University in Greeley.

Or maybe all his melancholy stemmed from the return of Taylor Bowen, the love of his life. "Damn."

He wadded up the paper towel and tossed it into the wastebasket, then glanced at the clock on his wall.

Barely noon and he was virtually done for the day. Maybe he should go home and get his fishing pole. If Ryan wasn't in school, he'd take him along.

He opened his office door and headed down the hall to Sue's desk. He could take up golf. Of course, the nearest golf course was thirty miles away. Raking his fingers through his hair, he decided to take his Jeep over to Miller's for an overdue checkup. Of course, he should probably go to Denver and shop for a new car instead.

Parting with his Jeep would be like losing a limb. All right, so he was overdramatizing, but the bottom line was, he loved that Jeep. He didn't want a new one. Miller's it would be.

"No emergencies?" he asked, noticing the empty waiting room.

"Nope, you're a free man." Sue gave him an impish grin. "Taylor had Mrs. Johnson first thing this morning."

Gordon refused to discuss Taylor with Sue. Last night had been humiliating enough already. "Well, I'll have my pager on. Hank's coming in this afternoon. Tell him I'll be back around three to check my post-op patients. Later."

"Wait, we have an animal control problem," Sue said, but he kept walking.

Ignoring Sue's stunned expression, Gordon deposited his lab coat in his office and headed out the back door. The sun was shining and it promised to be a beautiful summer day. No reason to waste it sitting around an office where he wasn't needed. He loosened his collar, stripped off his tie, and removed the ragtop from his beloved Jeep.

Miller's Garage was only a few blocks away. Of course, everything in Digby proper was only a few blocks. He swung into the drive and pulled the parking brake, but before he could kill the engine, it sputtered and died a lingering death. Patting the steering wheel, he said, "Sorry I've been neglecting you, Henrietta."

A sleek but dusty BMW pulled in beside his Jeep and a yuppie of the highest order climbed out. *Hmm, he must be lost.*

"Excuse me?" the yuppie said.

"Yes?" Gordon climbed from his Jeep and stood there, waiting for the yuppie to ask for directions.

"Is . . . *this* Dugby?"

Distaste edged the man's voice and made Gordon bristle. "It's *Digby.* Were you looking for it?"

The man looked down at a piece of paper in his hand. "Yes. Unfortunately." He looked around again, then approached Gordon. "Can you tell me how to find this place?"

Gordon's cheeks burned. "The Digby Veterinary Clinic?" What did this yuppie want with his clinic? He didn't have an animal in the car.

"Yes, my fiancée is practicing medicine there, if you can believe *that.*"

Gordon's teeth clenched and he drew a deep breath through his nose. "Fiancée?"

"Yes. Do you know where I can find this place?"

Gordon noted the perfect hair, the perfect suit,

the perfect face. From Taylor's perfect life. The guy smelled like money, too. *Yeah, perfect.*

Clearing his throat, he thrust out his hand, surprised by the firmness of the yuppie's handshake. "Gordon Lane, the local veterinarian."

The man eyed Gordon with renewed interest. "Then you must know Dr. Bowen."

"Yeah, you could say that." Gordon forced a smile. "I'll bet you're Jeremy Cole."

"Right you are, and isn't it fortuitous that I ran into you here?"

*Just my luck.* "I just left the clinic. Taylor was with a patient."

"Perhaps she'll be finished by the time I get there."

"I thought you weren't coming until tomorrow." Gordon struggled to keep accusation from entering his tone. "She, uh, mentioned it."

"Of course." Jeremy flicked a piece of lint from his sleeve. "The company jet reached Denver earlier in the day, so I rented a car and drove up today instead of in the morning." He glanced at the paper in his hand again. "Though it seems to me these directions could've been a lot more direct."

Gordon glanced at the paper Jeremy held out to him, immediately recognizing Sue's handiwork. "Remind me to draw you a new map for the trip back." He unbuttoned his cuffs and rolled up his sleeves. "Just head down Digby Boulevard two blocks, then turn right on Drumond. The clinic is on the left."

"Great, thanks." Jeremy waved as he headed

around to the driver's side of his rented car. "I'm sure we'll see each other again during my stay."

"Sure." Gordon waited until the BMW was out of sight, then turned and leaned on Henrietta's hood with both hands. That rich yuppie-dweeb was what Taylor wanted in her life. Not a small-town vet. She wanted to do research, and Dr. Cole obviously had the money and contacts to back her.

Gordon stared long and hard at the Jeep, ran his hands along the faded paint. A lump formed in his throat. He'd clung to the past for too damned long. It was way past time to let go of this piece of junk.

And Taylor Bowen.

# TEN

Sue looked over the list of activities she had planned for Jeremy Cole and shook her head. Just reading it exhausted her.

Horseback riding, rafting, hiking, a *frijole* sculpting contest, a Bluegrass Festival, and a visit to the Florissant Fossil Beds would keep him busy. Jeremy would definitely not be bored, nor would he have time to spend with Taylor. Besides, Ryan would enjoy all the activity. School wouldn't be out for another three weeks, but this would be like summer vacation.

All rolled into one three-day weekend.

The front door opened and she looked up with a scowl, expecting another drop-in patient. Instead, one of the handsomest men she'd ever seen strolled through the door. *Hello.*

He was impeccably dressed in a dark blue suit and red tie. His hair was wavy and almost black, with one curl falling rakishly across his forehead. Her heart did a little flutter as he approached, flashing a million-dollar smile.

"Good afternoon," he said in a smooth, deep voice.

"Good afternoon." Sue straightened and returned his smile. "What can I do for you?" *Oh, please let me do something for you.* It wasn't every day a guy walked through the door from the front cover of *GQ*. Okay, so that never happened in Digby.

"I'm Dr. Cole. Jeremy Cole?"

"Oh. *Oh.*" Sue leapt to her feet and shook his hand. "I'm Sue Wheeler. We spoke on the phone yesterday, and I sent you the fax." She paused, trying to reconstruct their conversation. "I thought you were coming tomorrow."

"Change in plans." Jeremy smiled again. "Is Taylor here?"

"No, she just left for lunch." *Thank goodness.* Sue turned over the piece of paper containing Jeremy's itinerary. "Taylor's been working very hard since she got here."

"I'm sure." He looked around. "It's quite clean for a, uh, veterinary clinic."

Sue bit back her retort. The guy needed some enlightenment. Otherwise, he wasn't bad. For her, though—not for Taylor. Definitely wrong for Taylor.

"Since Taylor's been so busy, she asked me to arrange some activities for this weekend," she explained, crossing her fingers behind her back. "We wouldn't want you getting bored on your first visit."

"Ah, I see." He frowned, his brow furrowing; then he met her gaze again, his chocolate-brown eyes sweeping the length of her.

Heat oozed slowly through Sue and she smiled again. "I'd better call the bed-and-breakfast and find out if they can take you a day earlier than planned."

She reached for the phone book, hoping old Mrs. Llewellyn wouldn't blow this one despite all of Sue's coaching. After punching the number in, she waited for an answer, but the voice mail came on instead.

"Mrs. Llewellyn," Sue said, ignoring the recording's instructions, "Jeremy Cole is here a day early and—" She smiled at Jeremy, who was still staring at her with those incredible eyes. "Oh, a skunk? How dreadful. No, I understand. Yes, I'll give Dr. Cole your apologies. Thanks." She hung up the phone and summoned her best storytelling abilities for the whopper she was about to impart.

"I gather there's a problem?" Jeremy quirked a brow, making her want to reach up and brush that stray curl away.

"Yes, I'm afraid so." Sue drew a deep breath, trying to remember all her well-laid plans. She hadn't bargained on Jeremy being quite so handsome. Flustered, she closed the phone book and returned it to her desk drawer, crossing her fingers behind her back again. "A skunk got into the cellar at the bed-and-breakfast, and they've had to close for fumigation."

"Well, I'll just have to stay with Tay—"

"Nonsense. I have a guest room, and this will make it easier for us to get to all our activities this weekend."

"But what about Taylor's house?"

"Hey, there's no furniture in her guest room, and I won't take no for an answer," she pressed, praying that Ryan and Patches hadn't been playing in that room. "I'll turn on the answering service and we'll head over there right now and get you settled."

Jeremy shook his head. "I think I should talk to Taylor before you go to so much trouble."

"No trouble at all." Sue waved her fingers and retrieved her purse. "Besides, Taylor's on call all weekend. You'll barely get to see her."

"Oh, I didn't realize . . ." Jeremy sighed and shoved his hands into his pockets. "I guess I have no choice but to take you up on your kind offer."

"That's right." Sue gave him what she hoped was her sexiest smile. "You don't."

*And I have no choice but to believe in love at first sight.*

The weekend was slow. No emergencies . . . and no Jeremy. Taylor spent her hours at the house, waiting for Jeremy to call. He'd come to see her, but he was with Sue.

Sue. The woman who'd destroyed Taylor's relationship with Gordon. Wasn't one man from Taylor's life enough for Sue?

However, when Sunday morning came and Jeremy finally called Taylor to make a breakfast date, she realized how relieved she was not to have had him underfoot all weekend. It was time to tell Jeremy they had no future.

She met him at Gertie's Diner, where he announced plans for white-water rafting that afternoon. His eyes glowed with excitement, and he was wearing jeans, hiking boots, and a denim shirt. She'd never seen this side of him before.

He rattled on for forty-five minutes about all the adventures Sue and Ryan had taken him on this weekend. Taylor was amazed, and not a bit jealous. The reserved, impeccably groomed yuppie had vanished, and the transformation was all positive.

"Jeremy, I'm glad you're having a good weekend," she said, reaching for her coffee and taking a sip. "It was kind of Sue to fill in for me while I'm on call." And Taylor couldn't help but wonder about Sue's motives. Of course, Jeremy was attractive. Perhaps it was nothing more than that.

"The only time I've ever been to the Rockies before was skiing in Aspen." He shook his head and raked his fingers through his hair, mussing it nicely. "This has been an incredible experience. Once I adjusted to the altitude, that is." His cheeks reddened.

*Jeremy Cole blushing?* He seemed so human. Taylor felt comfortable with him, but seeing him again reconfirmed the fact that he wasn't the right man for her. Even though he could help her get the research grant she'd always wanted, the thought of marrying him left her cold. She couldn't prostitute herself that way.

"So have you given any more thought to letting me buy out your contract?"

His question caught her off-guard and she chewed the inside of her cheek as she contemplated her answer. "It would be wrong to leave Digby without a doctor, Jeremy," she said carefully. "I won't do that."

"Taylor, I—"

"No, wait." She reached across the table and gave his hand a squeeze. "I have to tell you something else."

"All right, I'm listening."

She still couldn't get over the change in him, and she hoped it was permanent. "I've given us a lot of thought, and—"

"We aren't right for each other," he finished, giving her a cockeyed grin. "But we're still friends, and I think your gifts are being wasted up here."

Stunned was an understatement. Taylor struggled for a few minutes to regain her composure. Letting Jeremy down easy had been far easier than she'd ever imagined. "How . . . long have you known?"

He shook his head and chuckled. "Probably a long time, but this visit has made me realize a lot of things." He drew a deep breath. "I like it here, and I'm going to stay in Denver for a while to check out some things for Dad. Do you mind if I visit again?"

"Mind?" A pleasing warmth stole through her that had nothing to do with physical attraction. Friendship. Jeremy Cole was much more appealing as a friend than a potential lover. "I'd love for you to visit, and I'll give you my brother's number in Denver. I'll give him a call and I'll bet he can show you around."

"I'd like that." He smiled again. "Funny, before I flew out here, I planned on taking you back with me, kicking and screaming if necessary."

"And now . . . ?"

He gave a nervous laugh. "I like it better this way. It feels . . . right."

"Yeah, it does." Taylor relaxed for the first time since Jeremy's phone call at the clinic. Her pager beeped and she retrieved it from her purse. "Excuse me a minute. Cell phones don't work up here in the mountains, so I'll just use the pay phone."

She spotted Sue and Ryan coming through the front door of the diner as she made her way past the infamous unisex rest room to the phone. After punching in the number displayed on her pager, she watched Sue and Ryan slide into the booth with Jeremy.

They looked good together. Really good. A smile curved her lips just as a woman's frantic voice answered the phone.

"Dr. Bowen here, returning your call?" Taylor said.

"Thank God," the woman said. "This is Laura Kenner. My little boy fell out of a tree and I'm afraid his arm's broken."

Taylor asked a few questions and determined that there was no bleeding, and the boy's father had already immobilized the injured arm. Taylor instructed them to meet her at the clinic so she could get an X ray.

She'd never used Gordon's X ray equipment, so she dialed his number next. He sounded sexy and drowsy, and her hormones darned near burst into song. *Down, girl.* "Gordon, I have a patient meeting me at the clinic in a few minutes." She described the situation, and apologized for not having him show her the X ray equipment during regular office hours. He ignored her apology and agreed to meet her.

She turned to make her way back to the table and found it empty. Jeremy had left cash for their bill and a scribbled note of apology for leaving. She smiled again, satisfied that the Jeremy problem was resolved permanently.

As she drove the short distance to the clinic, she thought about her instantaneous and stimulating response to the sound of Gordon's voice over the phone this morning. She'd never responded that way to Jeremy, even when he'd kissed her. Sadness settled in her heart like a hunk of cold lead.

Would she *ever* feel that way about another man?

"Damn." She parked her VW behind the clinic and unlocked the back door. Flipping on lights as she went, she unlocked the front door and propped it open with a wedge of wood so the Kenners would know to come inside.

They arrived a few minutes later. Little Adam Kenner was a four-year-old heartbreaker with a head full of blond curls and a cherubic, tearstained face. Taylor asked Mr. Kenner to put his son on the exam table, then removed the towel they'd tied around the boy's waist to hold his arm stationary. Adam's sobbing grew louder.

"I know this hurts," she said gently, feeling his fingers and lifting his sleeve to expose his upper arm, "but we have to see how badly you're hurt."

"Can you give him something?" Mrs. Kenner asked, her lower lip trembling. "I'd rather have my own arm broken than see my baby hurt."

"Not until I see the X ray," she said. "If the bone has to be set, we won't want anything in his stomach. It won't be long now, though."

"It's set up in here," Gordon said from the doorway.

She hadn't even heard him come in. "Thanks." The Kenners followed her and Gordon down the hall to X ray.

"Hey, Adam," Gordon said in a cheery voice, "how's that mutt of yours doing?"

"F-fine," the boy said, sniffling.

"Well, that's how you're going to be, too." Gordon swung the X ray machine away from the table. "You're the first human ever to have your picture taken here. That makes you pretty special, I think."

Adam nodded and whimpered as his father lifted him to the table. Taylor showed Gordon which bones she needed X rayed and let him talk her through the process with his equipment.

She sent the Kenners and Adam back to the exam room while she and Gordon processed the film. He clipped the X rays on the viewer and flipped on the light. There were two breaks, but neither involved a joint. Even so, she decided to put a temporary cast on and send them to a specialist in Buena Vista first thing in the morning.

Mr. Kenner questioned Taylor's decision and turned to Gordon. "What do you think about this?" he asked.

Taylor's patient wanted a second opinion from the local vet? She controlled her anger and drew a deep breath as she measured the correct dose of a liquid pain medication for Adam.

"Bill, I'm just a veterinarian, but I know one thing for sure."

Taylor watched Adam's mother give her son the

medication, trying to ignore the conversation between the two men. She failed.

"Your son is lucky Dr. Bowen was here to treat him and she's doing exactly what I would've done for your retriever."

Taylor looked up and saw Gordon's grin, his aqua eyes twinkling. Her heart stuttered and raced forward at an alarming rate.

Mr. Kenner gave a nervous laugh and shook his head. "Beg pardon, Dr. Bowen," he said. "I meant no offense."

"None taken." Taylor smiled and took the empty medicine cup from Mrs. Kenner. "This medication will start working fast; then we'll get that temporary cast in place." She stooped in front of Adam and said, "Your arm won't hurt as bad once the cast is on. Do you want a red, green, or blue one?"

"Blue."

Gordon assisted, handing her materials and equipment as needed. Her hand brushed against his more than once, sending rivulets of desire oozing through her each time. By the time she sent the Kenners on their way with pain medication and instructions to get Adam through the night, in addition to the specialist's phone number, she was incredibly agitated.

After locking the front door, she returned to the exam room to clean up the mess, but Gordon had beaten her to it. "Thank you," she said.

"You're welcome." He smiled. "You're good with patients."

His praise warmed her far more than it should've. "Thank you. So are you."

He flashed her one of his boyish grins and her head spun. "I obtained EMT certification shortly after I returned to Digby."

She nodded. "That's right. You've been the only medical care in town for a long time."

"Only for emergencies, but if you hadn't been here, the Kenners would've had to drive Adam to Buena Vista in pain." He tossed some gauze into the trash and looked around the room. "All done."

He pinned her with his gaze. Taylor stood paralyzed, drowning in the intensity of his eyes. She wanted desperately to cover the distance between them and lean her cheek against his shoulder. Her breathing quickened and she trembled.

He took a few steps toward her, then closed his eyes. "No, forget that," he whispered.

"What?"

"I seem to have a problem keeping my hands to myself lately." His voice sounded husky and strained.

"I . . . is . . ."

"Well, we'd better get out of here before someone decides the clinic is open Sundays now."

She wanted to ask him why it was a problem that he couldn't keep his hands to himself but clenched hers into fists instead. "I locked the front door."

"All my patients went home Friday evening, so even Hank isn't here tonight." Gordon walked past her and into the hall. "I just want to make sure everything's locked up tight."

Taylor nodded, turning off the light as she followed him from the room. He walked around the waiting room, checked the locks and shades, and flipped off that light, too. "All set," he announced.

"Thank you again for meeting me here."

"No problem." A cynical tone edged his voice. "You're free to go back to your fiancé now."

"My *what?*" She was too tired for this. "I don't have one." And that had been true even before her conversation with Jeremy this morning.

"A man who'd come all this way to see you is serious, Taylor." Gordon's features seemed pinched, as if he was in great pain. "Trust me."

"We were never engaged. Besides, he's busy gallivanting all over the Rockies with Sue." She folded her arms across her abdomen. "And he's staying at her house. Did you know that?"

Surprise made Gordon's brows arch upward. "I believe Sue has an ulterior motive."

Taylor nodded. "I agree, though I'm not sure that's still true." She pivoted and headed toward the back door. "Thanks again for helping out with my patient, Gordon. I'll see you tomorrow."

Blinking back the scalding sensation behind her eyes, Taylor opened the back door and stepped into the late afternoon sunshine. Something shiny and red was parked beside her yellow VW. "What . . . ?"

Gordon closed the door behind them and locked it. "Brand-new Jeep," he said. "Like it?"

"Henrietta's . . . gone?" She spun around to face him, surprised by how much this bothered her. "You loved that old Jeep, Gordon." *I loved that old Jeep.* "Why?"

He lifted a shoulder and his nostrils flared slightly.

"Henrietta was breaking down every other day. I haven't bought this one yet, but I'm test-driving it for the weekend. Not sure about the color, though."

On rubbery legs, she followed him down the steps, where they both stood staring at the brand-new Jeep. "But . . . what about Henrietta?" she asked again as he opened her car door.

After she was in the driver's seat, she rolled down the window to stare at him. His lips pressed into a thin line and he shook his head. "Time to put the past where it belongs."

He walked away and climbed into his brand-new, very red, very *un*-Gordon Jeep. She watched him start the engine and back out of the parking lot. He waved, then drove down Drumond without a backward glance.

Taylor stared at her stricken face in her rearview mirror. *Time to put the past where it belongs.*

"Like me?"


Tuesday evening came way too fast. Taylor's doorbell rang promptly at seven, and she drew a deep breath before opening it. Sue looked nervous standing there, clutching a bottle of wine in one hand and balancing a pizza box in the other.

A healthy dose of déjà vu smacked Taylor right between the eyes. How many times during her life had Sue rung this very doorbell? She swallowed the lump in her throat and took the pizza box as her guest came inside.

"Looks like we're in for more rain," Sue said, pausing to stare at the piano. "Is that—"

"Yeah." Taylor closed the front door and stood beside Sue, staring at the piano. And remembering. "Mom's."

"Remember when we used to play duets on this thing?"

Taylor smiled. "Mom had the patience of a saint."

"And your dad had earplugs."

They both laughed nervously, and Taylor headed for the kitchen. "Let's eat before this gets cold."

"Where's the corkscrew?" Sue asked, setting the bottle of wine on the counter.

"Uh, I'm not sure." Taylor shrugged. "Haven't needed one since I got here."

"Drawer number . . . three." Sue opened the third drawer down and said, "Bingo."

Taylor set the table with plates, napkins, and wineglasses while Sue opened the wine. They sat across from each other in awkward silence.

"Jeremy told me you want to do some kind of medical research." Sue reached for a piece of pizza. "What kind of research?"

Small talk was safe. "Immunology. Mom's asthma gets worse every year, and she's been getting allergy shots for years."

"Like Patches."

"What?" Taylor knew the easy stuff wouldn't last, but she appreciated having time to warm up to Sue's presence in her home and in her life again. "Is that what's wrong with Patches?"

"Gordon has run the gamut of tests, but the dog

is healthy." She shrugged. "We're convinced it's an allergy that makes him have these attacks, especially in cold weather."

"Wheezing?"

"Right. Asthma." Sue gave Taylor a sad smile. "Maybe your folks should move back to the mountains. It might help your mom's asthma."

"It might." Taylor leaned back and fiddled with her napkin. "Anyway, I hope my research will find ways to help people with allergies. Hey, why don't we do some scratch tests on Patches? It couldn't hurt and it might work. I don't know if that's ever done with dogs, but why not?"

"Suits me." Sue lowered her gaze to her untouched pizza.

"I know what you want to talk about," Taylor began, reaching for the open bottle and pouring them both a generous amount of merlot. "And it isn't necessary."

Sue squared her shoulders and lifted her glass in a toast. "Here's to truth, whether you want to hear it or not."

Taylor's stomach clenched and she took a sip of wine. "Mmm, good."

"All right, you drink and I'll talk." Sue sipped her wine. "Better yet, we'll both drink and I'll talk."

Resigned, Taylor reached for a slice of pizza. "All right, you obviously aren't going to take no for an answer, so have at it."

"Thanks." Sue took another sip and wrapped her hands around the stem of her glass and stared at

Taylor. "When I told you I was pregnant with Gordon's child, I truly believed that was true."

Taylor struggled for a deep breath and finally found one, then released it very slowly. "Well, that was direct." She'd never doubted Sue's sincerity, which was exactly why she'd been so crushed, and why she hadn't confronted Gordon before leaving Digby. "I never thought you were lying, Sue, so this discussion really isn't necessary."

"Yes, it is." Sue took another sip and cleared her throat. When she met Taylor's gaze again, her eyes sparkled with unshed tears.

"Don't you dare cry, Sue Wheeler." Taylor took a huge gulp of wine and coughed. "Anything but tears."

"No promises." Sue's voice warbled dangerously. "But I'll try. Just hush up and listen. This is hard. I tried to convince Gordon that he should talk to you, but men are so stupid sometimes."

*Not to mention stubborn.* Despite everything, Taylor still felt that invisible bond she and Sue had always shared. She'd missed their friendship much more than she'd realized. "Go on. I'm listening."

"Thanks." Sue sniffled and released a long sigh. "You remember graduation night. Everybody under twenty in Digby was three sheets to the wind by midnight." She took another sip of merlot and shook her head. "I'm afraid I was a lot farther gone than that, and *very* unaccustomed to alcohol."

Taylor took a bite of pizza and chewed. It stuck in her constricting throat and she washed it down with more wine. The alcohol warmed her, despite the ghosts of the past trying to break down the door to her mental vault.

"That was the night I had sex for the first time." Sue gave a self-deprecating laugh, then sobered and leveled her probing gaze on Taylor. "Problem is, I don't remember who with."

"What . . . are you saying?" Taylor went cold. No, arctic. "You told me it was Gor—"

"Wait." Sue squeezed her eyes shut and held her hand up in front of her. "Please, just listen."

Anger burned in Taylor's chest. Now she *needed* to know the truth. All of it. "I'm *listening.*"

"I remember having sex. Sort of. I know it happened, though I can't remember details." Sue's voice shook. "And I remember Gordon driving me home. He had to pull over for me to throw up twice."

Taylor rubbed the back of her neck and reached for the wine bottle. Good thing she'd bought a bottle earlier in the day, because they were probably going to need it. She refilled both their glasses and drew a deep breath.

"So that was why you believed Gordon was . . . the one?" Taylor took a mouthful of wine and tried to savor the fruity flavor rolling over her tongue. Anything to keep from thinking about . . . "Gordon was with *me* that night, Sue. He brought me home late. I remember being worried that my folks would be mad."

"He . . . he told me later that he found me sitting on the curb in front of your house after he walked you to the door." Sue laughed again without a trace of humor. "The bottom line is, I got so drunk I can't remember who I slept with, let alone how I ended up at your house." Her lower lip quivered. "The next day, I only remembered that I'd had sex and that Gordon took me home. I assumed . . ." She shrugged. "Taylor, I'm so sorry."

Taylor stared at Sue over the rim of her wineglass. She believed Sue. Again. Believed her completely. "Later that summer, when you found out you were pregnant, you really believed it was Gordon's child."

Sue nodded slowly. "You know I did." She dabbed her eyes with her napkin. "I was terrified and you were my best friend."

"Yeah," Taylor whispered. "Who else were you going to tell?"

Sue's face crumpled and tears rolled in full force now. "I'm sorry, but I'm going to c-cry whether you like it or not."

Taylor stood and grabbed the box of tissues off the counter and placed it on the table beside Sue. "When did you realize the baby wasn't Gordon's?"

"I didn't know you would *leave.*" Sue's voice was barely more than a whisper. "I figured we'd both talk to Gordon and work it out somehow."

It was Taylor's turn to laugh. "Color me cynical, Sue, but I wasn't real crazy about Gordon *or you* at the time."

"No, I suppose not." Sue took a sip of wine and sniffled. "I had to tell my folks about the baby, and they demanded to know who the father was."

"And you named Gordon." Mother had tried to talk to Taylor about this long after they'd all moved away, but she'd refused to listen. "Then what happened?"

"Dad went berserk and confronted Gordon and his folks." Sue shook her head. "It was ugly."

"I'll bet Gordon offered to marry you anyway." She gave Sue a sad smile. "Didn't he?"

"Yes, even after he told us he couldn't be the father." Sue reached for another tissue and blew her nose. "After you left, he offered to marry me. My parents wanted me to do it, but I couldn't." She met Taylor's gaze again. "I thought . . . you'd come home. I really did. I wrote dozens of letters, but you never answered."

"I . . . I never opened them."

"Oh, Taylor." Sue's eyes mirrored Taylor's anguish. "And I've lived with the guilt of knowing what I did to you and Gordon all this time."

"But you didn't know he wasn't the father when you told me." Taylor rolled her eyes. "And *I* didn't trust Gordon." She closed her eyes and smacked the table. "God, why didn't I *trust* him?"

"That's the part I feel worst about." Sue reached for Taylor's hand. "You didn't trust Gordon, because you *did* trust m-me. Your b-best friend."

Sue buried her face in her hands and sobbed. Anger, confusion, and betrayal battled within Taylor, but Sue's tears overruled everything for supremacy. After a few moments, Taylor found herself holding Sue while they both cried. All the tears she'd been holding back poured out, leaving her spent and shaken.

If only she'd talked to Gordon, or opened Sue's letters, or listened to her mother. . . . She'd worn her self-righteous anger like a suit of armor, and for what? Nothing. None of that mattered now.

Finally, she patted her best friend's—yes, her best friend's—shoulder and grabbed two tissues, handing one to Sue. "No more tears," Taylor said, returning to her chair and her wine. "You've blamed yourself all these years, but it really wasn't your fault."

"Yes, it—"

"No." Taylor drew a shaky breath. "It's all *my* fault for running away. What a coward. I was the wronged one, so I thought. God, when I think how much I must've hurt Gordon . . ."

"His heart was broken." Sue tilted her head to one side. "It still is."

Taylor drank her wine, remembering the look on Gordon's face when he'd practically made love to her at the clinic. He'd wanted to talk to her, but they'd ended up tearing at each other's clothes instead.

"I have to talk to him," she finally said.

"Then you can be together again." Sue brightened.

"I wish it was that simple." Taylor's heart pressed against her throat. "He'll never be able to trust me again."

"Trust is important to Gordon." Sue reached across the table and squeezed Taylor's hand. "But he loves you, and I believe he'll forgive you. After all, I think you just forgave me."

Taylor nodded. "You made a mistake. What's not to forgive?" *And why'd it take me so damn long to listen?*

"I've never had another friend like you, Taylor." Sue gave her a weak smile. "I've missed you."

"I've missed you, too." Taylor exhaled very slowly. "I've hurt everybody, including myself."

"I should've found a way to make you listen years ago."

"Too stubborn." Taylor chuckled. "Well, whether or not it changes the way Gordon feels about me, I have to talk to him." She cleared her throat and rubbed her eyes. "When and how, though?"

"That's easy," Sue said, lifting her glass. "Just do it."

"Great." Taylor rolled her eyes. "You're a big help. So when should I just 'do it?'"

Sue's expression grew intense and she leaned closer. "During the full moon, of course."

# ELEVEN

Ryan didn't like this. Not one bit. Not only had Dr. Cole spent the weekend at their house, but the dweeb had made his mother laugh and smile more than she had in years. Then, to top it all off, Ryan had walked into the kitchen and caught them kissing.

*Yuck.*

And Dr. Cole planned to come back again this weekend. Somehow, Ryan had to prevent that.

His band teacher had just dropped him off after the field trip, and Mom had gone back to bed after letting him into the house. He didn't have school today, so now Ryan stood at his bedroom window staring out at the morning sky.

Gordon was supposed to marry his mom and be his new dad, not Jeremy Cole. Gordon should be the one to make her laugh and smile. And, yes, even kiss her.

*Yuck.*

Patches whimpered near his feet and Ryan bent down to scratch the mutt behind the ears. "It's all *her* fault." His gaze swept the room and fell on the handle of his track-maker sticking out from beneath his bed. If he could make Dr. Bowen leave Digby, that rich dweeb wouldn't have any reason to come back for another visit.

Mrs. Lane had told Ryan how frightened Dr. Bowen was of bears. This week, there would be a lot more bear tracks at her house.

A whole lot more.

The doorbell rang shortly after dawn, and Taylor opened one eye. Her tongue felt as if it was coated with fur, and the pulse in her head was doing the rumba.

*My God, I have a hangover.*

Wincing, she struggled to a sitting position and remembered that she and Sue had finished one bottle of wine and made a healthy dent in a second. Sue had called a neighbor to drive her home, refusing to stay the night, so she'd be home when Ryan returned from his field trip this morning.

The bell sounded again, and didn't it seem louder this time? Groaning, she dragged herself out of bed and pulled on her robe. She reached the front door just as the bell rang a third time.

"I'm coming. Oh." She grabbed her head with both hands. The sound of her voice made her skull feel as if it would explode. " 'Physician, heal thyself,' " she whispered.

She pushed aside the curtain on the window beside the door and blinked. Why was Rick Miller standing on her front porch at this ungodly—

"Oh, no." She'd arranged for him to pick up her

car this morning for a tune-up. "Just a second." She grabbed her purse and took her car key off the ring, then opened the door. "I'm sorry, Rick. I forgot."

His shock at her appearance was evident. "Wild night?" He flashed her a grin. "Last time I had a hangover was after your high school graduation. It's hell when your only vice turns on you. Mike, Sue, and I were polluted. I don't even remember getting home that night." He pointed a finger at her. "Tomato juice with Tabasco sauce. It'll either cure you or kill you."

Was the cause of her condition that obvious? "Gee, thanks, Rick." She handed him the key. "Call me when the car's done?"

"Sure thing, Doc." He headed down the walk with her key, then called back over his shoulder, "Remember, tomato juice and Tabasco."

Wincing again, she closed the door. The mere thought of tomato juice made her stomach lurch, and she refused to even consider Tabasco sauce. She glanced at the clock, then headed toward the kitchen and coffee. Definitely not tomato juice.

Forty-five minutes, half a pot of coffee, and one shower later, she stood in the living room again, feeling almost human. A green knit top tucked into her jeans would be dressy enough for Digby once she put her lab coat over it. She grabbed her medical bag, strapped on a fanny pack in lieu of her purse, and tied a sweater around her waist. The clinic was a short walk away, and the morning air should help clear her head more. The aspirin she'd taken wouldn't hurt either.

The fog had cleared from her brain and she remembered what Rick had said about being out with Sue on graduation night. The night Ryan was conceived.

"Oh." She shook her head. Rick had been here all along, and he would've come forward if he was Ryan's father. That didn't make sense. Of course, he said he didn't even remember getting home that night.

And he'd mentioned Mike, too. She made a mental note to call her brother later and ask him what he remembered about that night. Ryan deserved to know who his father was, and Sue would have closure. Maybe Mike knew who Sue'd been with.

Taylor opened the door and saw someone moving around the yard. Quickly, she closed it again and peered through the window instead. Ryan Wheeler had a long stick with something attached to the end of it. He hurried around her yard, pressing the object into the ground at regular intervals.

"What the devil are you up to?" She waited until he climbed onto his bike and rode away with the long stick balanced across his handlebars. "Only one way to find out."

Taylor headed outside and locked the door behind her, then approached the area where Ryan had been. Bear prints. Dozens and dozens of bear prints.

No, *fake* bear prints. "You little snot." She walked around, noting that the tracks started and stopped in her yard. She'd been too terrified before to explore, or she might've realized that only a flying bear could've performed such a feat. "You little snot," she repeated, wondering why Ryan Wheeler was trying to terrorize her.

Of course, since her car was gone, he must've thought she'd already left for the clinic. Laughing quietly, Taylor wondered what Sue would think of her son's activities. Had he also drained Taylor's gas tank? But why?

She should talk to Sue. Who was she kidding? Gordon Lane had been waiting over a decade for her to talk to him. First things first. Besides, he'd been a little boy once upon a time. Maybe he would understand Ryan. Besides, she needed an excuse to talk to him. Alone.

And set things straight between them, once and for all.

Taylor headed back to the house to call Rick Miller. Her tune-up would have to wait for another day. She should be able to catch Gordon at home this morning and still get to the clinic before her first appointment.

Clouds rolled in again as she drove her Bug up the twisting mountain road toward Gordon's cabin. Thunder rumbled and lightning flashed. June was often cool and rainy in the high country. This year was no exception. The erosion along the roadside was much worse than usual.

A huge boulder suddenly appeared in the road and she swerved to miss it. Glancing up the mountainside, she weighed her options. She should turn around and go back, but it was time to settle things with Gordon. Past time.

Adrenaline spurred her to action. She slammed her car into first gear and hit the gas. Several seconds later, she was at the crest of the hill. She stopped and looked behind her. A mountain of mud and boulders covered what had once been a road. Everything was still. Deathly still.

She rested her forehead against the steering wheel, commanding her pulse to slow. Then she looked behind her again. She hadn't imagined it. The road was completely gone, buried in mud and rock.

If she hadn't decided to proceed to Gordon's, her car could've been buried. With her in it.

Her hands trembled as she drove the rest of the way up the dead-end road, praying Gordon was home. She should've called first. What if he'd gone down to the clinic early this morning?

"Really stupid, Taylor." As she rounded the last curve, she breathed a sigh of relief. Two Jeeps were parked in front of Gordon's cabin. A shiny new blue one . . . and Henrietta.

She smiled, parking her car between the two Jeeps. Blue was much more suitable for Gordon than red. And he hadn't traded Henrietta. Did that mean he couldn't put the past behind him after all?

"Get a grip." She left her medical bag in the car and went to the door. Just as she lifted her hand to knock, the door swung open and Gordon stared at her with surprise and open suspicion in his eyes.

"Taylor?" He looked beyond her, as if expecting

to find someone else with her. "You drove up here alone?"

She nodded, remembering the wall of mud and rock. "There was a mud slide," she said quietly. "Road's gone."

A frown creased his brow. "You could've been *killed.*" He opened the door wider and gestured for her to come in. "I'll make some fresh coffee. You must've had a good reason to come all the way up here."

"Yes." *A long overdue apology.* She drew a deep breath and followed him inside. The furniture was spare and tasteful. A few antiques plus a giant denim-covered recliner occupied the main room. Max was curled up on a rug before the cold hearth. All in all, the place was very Gordon. She loved it.

*Love . . . ?*

"Oh, God," she murmured, and he turned to stare at her from the kitchen doorway. "Oh, God." She felt cold all over and her head spun. Was it the hangover or her close call with the mud slide? No, it was the truth doing this to her.

She lifted her gaze and met Gordon's; then she simply sat down in the middle of the floor with a rather undignified plop. He hurried over to her and stooped beside her.

"You okay?" He reached for her wrist and checked her pulse. "You're playing the 'Minute Waltz.' Let's get you to the kitchen and some warm coffee. I need to call Sue and tell her we're stranded, and the county about the road, or we'll never get out of here."

Taylor nodded numbly as he helped her up and

guided her to the kitchen. She felt lousy, shaky and weak. The warmth of his strong arm around her waist made her feel better and worse all at once.

She knew the cause of her malady, and it wasn't from too much wine or a near-death experience on the mountain road. No, it was something much more dangerous. Uncontrollable.

She was still in love with Gordon Lane.

Gordon held his breath until he had Taylor settled in a chair at his kitchen table. Even that brief physical contact with her made him too warm, too eager, too horny for his own good.

Why had she driven up here? She could've been killed by that mud slide. Thank God she was here and safe. He couldn't bear the thought of anything happening to her.

Reminded of that, he went to the phone and called the county to report the road blockage. Last time, it had taken them a week to clear the mess. In good weather, he could hike down the mountain without a road.

But now he had Taylor to worry about. Taylor to look at. Taylor to talk to. Taylor to want . . .

After being assured that the road would be cleared as soon as possible—whatever that meant—he called the clinic. A very groggy-sounding Sue answered. "Hey, Sue, I'm stranded again."

She sighed. "When are you going to move off that mountain so this won't happen anymore?"

"Never."

"Well, in the winter it's snow and now it's . . . what?"

"Mud slide." Gordon glanced at Taylor, who sat staring out the window that spanned the entire back of his cabin. He lowered his voice and said, "It almost got Taylor on her way up here."

"Taylor?" Sue's tone brightened considerably. "She's there? With you? Stranded?"

"Well, yeah, I guess you could say that." He cleared his throat, deciding Sue was far too pleased with this turn of events. "Anyway, I called the county, and they're supposed to get the road cleared as—"

"Soon as possible."

Gordon chuckled. "Right."

"I'll cancel your appointments and call Dr. Swensen in Buena Vista to take calls for Taylor, and Mt. Harvard Animal Hospital to cover for you."

"Thanks."

"Don't mention it."

Definitely too pleased. Thunder rumbled overhead and rain fell in sheets. He sighed. "If it ever stops raining, we'll hike down to town and I'll stay with Mom until the road's clear."

"No hurry," Sue said. "Everything here will keep until the slide is cleaned up."

"Hmm. I'll keep you posted."

"You do that, and make sure you don't try to come down the mountain until after the full moon."

"What?" Frowning, he shot a sidelong glance at Taylor, who was still staring out the window at the deluge. "What's so important about the moon?"

"Trust me on this, Gordon," Sue said emphatically. "It's very important that you and Taylor not leave there until after the full moon."

He chuckled and shook his head. "You're nuts, Sue. When is the full moon?" Taylor turned to look at him with a quizzical expression and he shrugged.

"It's . . . either tonight or tomorrow night. Your calendar here doesn't say." He heard papers shuffling. "Just don't try to come down the mountain until Friday. Promise?"

"I'm sure it'll take the county longer than that to get the road clear anyway," he said. "Besides, the way it's raining, they won't even be able to start clearing today."

"Good."

"Absolutely nuts."

"We aim to please. Take care of Taylor. 'Bye."

Gordon hung up the phone and scratched his chin, wondering what sort of insanity had its grip on Sue now. PMS was last week. He felt Taylor's gaze on him and gave her a sheepish grin.

"Sue's nuts," he said.

"A nice nut, though." Her smile and her eyes looked wistful.

*Something's different.* "Coffee's done. How do you take yours?" He opened the cabinet door and took down two white mugs, trying not to think about why and how Taylor was different.

"A little milk, if you have it. No sugar." Taylor rose and came to stand beside him.

He felt her warmth at his side, and something terrifying unfolded in his chest. Not only was he alone here with the only woman he'd ever really loved, but he couldn't shake the feeling that this was somehow right. Taylor looked good standing in his kitchen.

*Get over it, Lane.* Angry at himself, he whirled around and opened the refrigerator, then grabbed the milk carton. He turned around and found her watching him—staring, really. Her eyes were large and moist, her expression lost.

"What is it, Taylor?" he asked, suddenly worried that something was terribly wrong. "Why'd you drive up here this morning?"

She cleared her throat and took the milk carton from him, pouring a little into her cup. When she turned to face him again, she said, "I came to apologize."

He shook his head, trying to remember what she should be apologizing for. "I don't—"

"This may take a while." She sighed, and a sad smile curved her lips. "Shall we sit here or in the living room?"

"It's getting chilly," he said, swallowing the lump in his throat. "I'll light a fire." He poured coffee into both their cups, then led the way back to the living room. "I guess this is sort of a forced vacation."

"Hmm. Yes, it is." She sat on the braided rug before the hearth, the coffee mug clutched in both hands. She raised it to her lips and took a long, slow drink. "You make good coffee, Gordon."

She looked even better in this room than she had in his kitchen. Paralyzed, he stood staring at her for several seconds, then remembered the fire. He set his cup on an end table, then laid the fire and made sure the damper was open. A few moments later, he had a cheery blaze going.

"That feels nice," she said, bathed in the orange glow of the flames.

He should've taken his cup and sat in his recliner, but some invisible force prompted him to join her on the rug instead. "This rain seems to be settling in for the duration." He reached for his coffee and took a long drink, trying to ignore the voices in the back of his mind that were overjoyed to have Taylor Bowen here.

Alone.

She was so close. He could touch her if he wanted—and, oh, he really wanted—but he wouldn't. He'd vowed to put that—her—behind him.

"You didn't keep the red Jeep."

Startled from his reverie, he met her gaze again. The room was bathed in shadows, though it was late morning. Heavy clouds and fog shrouded the cabin, forming a cocoon of privacy so absolute that it stole his breath and ignited his blood.

"I . . . I didn't like the red one." He took another sip of coffee. "Blue suits me better."

"Yes, it does." She fell silent again.

He watched her staring at the flames, her expression solemn but intense. "And you kept Henrietta."

"Yeah. I couldn't part with her." He cleared his throat and continued to watch her, burning to reach out and touch her cheek where the firelight made her glow like a ripe peach. *Damn.* The thought of peaches reminded him of other things, and his blood flow followed his gaze south. Her breasts filled out her knit top nicely. Really nicely.

"Gordon, I came here to apologize."

"You said that already." His words sounded terse, though he was only angry at himself and his inability to control his thoughts around this woman. "I'm sorry. That didn't come out right."

Taylor took a sip of coffee. "It's all right. We've both waited a long time for this."

His heart pressed against his throat and his gut clenched. "For what?"

She leaned forward and placed her cup on an end table, her breasts straining against her shirt, making him ache to fill his hands with her, to taste her, to bury himself inside her again. *Get over it, Lane.*

Clenching his teeth, he put his empty cup on the table and draped his arms over his knees. He was so hard, this position pinched badly, but he figured the pain was what he deserved and might help bring his libido back under control.

"Why are you here, Taylor?" He turned to look at her. "Really?"

"To apologize." She turned to face him, tucking her legs beneath her.

"For what?"

She reached for his hand. His first impulse was to jerk it away, but she was so soft and warm and close. So Taylor. He couldn't bring himself to break the contact. "For what?" he repeated softly.

She closed her eyes for a moment, then reopened them to imprison him. Their green depths held him captive.

"For not trusting you."

He furrowed his brow, trying to follow her. "I'm sorry, but I don't know what you're—" He closed his eyes, then reopened them to search her face for an answer. "Sue."

Taylor nodded slowly, her lower lip trembling. "She came over last night and we talked."

He drew a shaky breath and held it, finally releasing it very slowly. "So now you know."

"Yes, and I know how wrong I was for not trusting you." Her voice quavered ominously. "I . . . should've—"

"Doesn't matter now, Taylor." He pulled his hand free of hers and stared at the flames. "Ancient history."

"It matters to me."

He tilted his head and looked at her. She looked vulnerable and desirable, which did nothing to abate his burgeoning lust. "Why does it matter now?"

And why couldn't he use his anger to control his desire? There really was no justice in the world. Why did he want a woman who'd wronged him like this?

"It matters to me because I . . ."

"Because why?" He met and held her gaze, reading her torment in her eyes. "Guilt?"

She nodded slowly. "That's part of it," she admitted. "I messed up so many things by not trusting you. If only I'd come and talked to you . . ."

He jerked his gaze away. The sense of betrayal he'd felt all those years ago returned with a vengeance, and he clenched his fists. After several deep breaths, he met her gaze again.

"I've never cared about anyone the way I cared for you, Taylor." He gripped his knees, struggling to keep his cool. She wanted the truth out in the open now, and he was determined to give it to her. All of it.

"I . . ." Her face crumpled and tears streamed down her cheeks.

"God, don't cry." He couldn't stand a crying woman. "Just . . . don't."

She mopped at her tears with her sleeve, then sniffled. "I'm sorry." She reached for his hand again, but he maintained his grip on his knees.

"I'm listening. Let's get this over with."

She left her hand covering his. He desperately wanted to grab her and haul her into his lap. He wanted to hold her to him so she could never leave again.

But she *would* leave. In three years.

"I was so hurt when Sue came to me and told me she was pregnant with your child," she continued. "If any other girl had told me such a tale, I never would've believed it. *Never.*"

He nodded, knowing that was true. "You just left. You . . ." He leveled his gaze on hers. "You didn't even say good-bye. You threw it all away without a backward glance."

"No, I never forgot." She shifted her weight until she knelt before him. "I never forgot."

His throat burned and his head pounded. He'd shed his tears for Taylor long, long ago, and he wasn't about to do it now. "All right, so you've apologized."

She reached out and touched his cheek, caressing

him with her fingertips. "I carried your face in my mind when I left," she whispered.

*Just shoot me now.*

He closed his eyes for a moment, remembering how he'd felt when he went to her house the day after she left. The expression on her mother's face when he'd begged her to tell him where Taylor had gone. The way her father had berated him for hurting his little girl.

None of that mattered now, but the fact that she'd left still mattered. She'd tossed their love aside. All she had to do was talk to him. He could have told her the truth, talked to Sue, and spared them all these years of heartache.

"You just left," he repeated, standing and shoving his hands into his pockets. "Not a word to me or Sue or anybody." He whirled around and pinned her with his gaze.

She staggered to her feet, holding her hands out to him beseechingly. "That's why I came here this morning, Gordon," she said, a tremor in her voice. "I'm sorry. I can't undo the past, but I want you to know that I'm sorrier for that than anything in my life."

Silent tears spilled from her incredible green eyes, and he had to clench his fists at his sides to stop himself from reaching for her. "All right, you're sorry." He looked away, unable to watch the pain in her expression a moment longer. He pulled his anger around him like a protective cloak, shielding himself from falling victim to her charms again. "You've apologized. Congratulations."

"I guess there's no hope of you ever forgiving me."

He whirled around to face her, disbelief nearly driving him to his knees. "Forgive you?"

She nodded, tears shimmering on her lashes and cheeks. "Never mind." With a sigh, she turned to face the hearth. "It's too much to ask."

Gordon continued to stare at her, the pain in his heart spreading. She'd broken his heart once, and he couldn't risk letting her do that again. Forgiving her would set him free. Then he could pretend none of it mattered anymore.

It was his only defense against the truth.

"I'll forgive you, Taylor," he whispered.

She snapped her head around to meet his gaze, her brow furrowing. "You will?"

"On one condition."

She took a step toward him, her eyes wide, her lips slightly parted. "What condition?"

"That you never mention any of this again."

Taylor had come here to apologize, and she'd done that. Now he was offering his forgiveness.

For a price.

Her soul.

He wanted to bury the past and pretend it had never happened, while she was filled with the need to examine and understand it. He'd known the truth all along, while she'd just learned it. How could he expect her to forget it all now?

For the first time since leaving Digby, she knew the boy she'd given her heart to hadn't betrayed her with her best friend. The horrible "truth" she'd carried in her heart all these years wasn't true at all. She couldn't ignore that.

"I was so wrong. So very, very wrong." She shook her head slowly. "But ignoring the past isn't the same as forgiving."

The expression on his face mirrored the pain in her heart. "Don't, Taylor," he whispered. "Don't resurrect all this. Let it go. It hurts too damn much, and we can't undo it."

"I want your forgiveness, Gordon." She swallowed the bile burning her throat. "But I want *real* forgiveness—not just you sweeping it all under the rug."

He chuckled low in his throat and bent to scratch Max behind the ears. The dog seemed oblivious to all the anguish in the room. "Is this the only reason you drove up here?"

Taylor remembered Ryan's morning activities and cleared her throat. "No, there's another reason."

"What?" Gordon grabbed a log and laid it on the fire. The hot embers flared to life, licking greedily at the new fuel.

"Ryan."

Gordon's eyes widened as he straightened and faced her. "What about Ryan?"

Taylor explained what she'd seen this morning, and Gordon laughed. "I don't think it's funny," she said.

"No, I don't suppose you do, but he's a ten-year-old boy." Gordon shrugged; then his expression grew solemn. "And . . ."

"And what?"

He sighed and scraped his hand through his hair. "He wants me to marry his mom and be his dad."

Taylor nodded slowly, her suspicions confirmed. "And he considers me a threat."

Gordon's mask fell into place again. "Maybe."

"Sue's interested in Jeremy."

Genuine surprise flared in his eyes. "Really? The yuppie? I thought you were engaged."

Taylor shook her head. "We weren't engaged, and we both realized it wasn't right." She sighed. "He seemed like a different person when I saw him on Sunday."

The lamp in the corner flickered and went out. "Electricity's out, and probably the phone," Gordon said, picking up the extension on his desk. "Yep. I'd better fire up the generator."

He left the room before Taylor could respond. Gordon had no intention of discussing anything with her. She walked to the window and stared out at the heavy clouds. A shiver chased itself through her and she wrapped her arms around herself for warmth.

One thing was for sure: Tonight would be the longest night of her life.

# TWELVE

Tonight would be the longest night of Gordon's life.

He turned on the radio in the kitchen so they could listen to the news and weather. From the sound of things, the storm was settling in for the duration.

"I can sleep in that big recliner in the living room," Taylor said as she helped him clear the table after dinner. "It's huge."

"No, you take the bedroom and I'll sleep in the recliner." He'd never bothered to buy a couch, but now he wished he had.

"I don't want to put you to any trouble," she said, rinsing the plates under running water.

He flipped off the radio and covered the salad with plastic wrap. He was trying to conserve generator fuel for important things like the refrigerator, so he retrieved two more kerosene lamps from the cabinet and made sure they were full and ready. One already burned on the kitchen table.

"No trouble. I like my recliner." He handed her a lamp. "There are matches in the tin on the dresser."

"Are you trying to get rid of me, Doctor?"

*Oh, yeah, definitely.* "Nope, but there's barely enough light to read by. Nothing to do but go to bed." He winced when he realized what he'd said.

She cleared her throat and blinked, staring at him for several seconds. "Gee, we could talk."

*No, anything but that.* Lightning struck somewhere nearby, and the floor rumbled beneath them.

"Gordon, we really need to talk."

He shook his head. "I'm in denial. Give me time to get used to this."

"Get used to me knowing the truth?" She shrugged. "You've known the truth all along, and I'm the one who just learned it."

"I don't want to discuss this. You made a choice not to learn the truth, and I'm making a choice not to discuss it now." He retrieved the burning lamp from the table and carried it into the living room. "I'd better stoke the fire. If the temperature drops much more, we'll have snow by morning."

"I remember having snow on the Fourth of July when I was a kid."

*The Fourth of July.* Did she remember their first time? Did she dream of that Fourth of July between their junior and senior years in high school? Did she remember every minute detail about what happened that day? What they'd shared? The promises they'd made?

He paused in front of the hearth and faced her. The expression on her face tore at him. She remembered. Joy mingled with terror in his heart and made him swallow hard. *Just don't talk about it, Taylor.* He couldn't stand that. Not now.

She brought her fingers to her lips, her eyes wide green pools. "I . . . remember the last time we spent Fourth of July together," she whispered.

"Don't." He set the lamp on the mantel and put more logs on the fire. "I'll get you a blanket, if you insist on sleeping out here."

She didn't answer, so he took that as agreement and carried his lamp into his bedroom and set it on his dresser. He opened the closet door and saw his Taylor box—the one containing pictures and that beach towel he'd kept all these years.

He doubled up his fist and slammed it into his palm. Why did everything have to remind him? Why was she here torturing him? Stranded with him?

Alone?

"Gordon?" she said from the doorway, startling him.

He reached onto the shelf and grabbed a blanket that had no sentimental meaning whatsoever, a pillow, and a pillowcase, then handed them to her.

"Your last chance to claim the bed," he said, forcing a tight smile.

"Got an old T-shirt I can borrow for a nightgown?"

Without a word, he grabbed a yellow T-shirt from a drawer and laid it on the pile in her arms.

"Thanks." Her gaze darkened and she pulled her lips into a thin line. "Go ahead and pretend for now," she said, lifting her chin a notch. "But by morning I want you to be ready to talk about this. I'm *not* taking no for an answer."

She whirled around and stomped into the next room, leaving Gordon alone with his memories.

He closed the door behind her and walked woodenly to the bed and threw himself facedown on it. The truth was, he wanted to forgive Taylor. Desperately. But he couldn't trust her.

If he allowed himself to trust her, she'd have the power to hurt him. No matter what, he couldn't give her that power ever again. But by denying her that power, he was also denying himself the very thing he wanted most.

With the door closed, the room grew frigid in no time. He undressed and climbed under the comforter, folding his arms behind his head. If he managed a wink of sleep tonight, it would be a miracle. He should've doused the lamp, but instead he kept staring at the patterns the flickering flame threw across the beamed ceiling.

The woman he wanted more than any other was in the next room. Why was he shivering alone in his bed?

*Because you're a fool.*

Hours passed and he dozed off and on, but his thoughts and his dreams kept straying to the woman in the next room. Was she sleeping? Was she wearing anything under his yellow T-shirt?

The thought made him harden and he grimaced in self-disgust. Would he ever stop wanting Taylor Bowen? "Damn."

The floor creaked just beyond his door, and he held his breath as the doorknob turned. His heart thundered in his chest and he wanted desperately to call out to her.

Slowly, the door opened, and she stood framed by

firelight. Her hair cascaded down around her shoulders in a mass of dark curls.

*Dear God.* His gaze drifted down the length of her, savoring every inch of bare leg exposed below his T-shirt. His body sprang to life, even as his mouth formed the words, "Taylor, don't . . ."

"I've been lying awake, and I can't stop remembering." She padded barefoot to his bed. "Look at me, Gordon."

He raised his lashes and met her gaze. Something bright and hot and dangerous burned in her eyes. "Do you know . . ." He bit the inside of his cheek to silence his words.

She put her knee on his bed and cupped his cheek with one hand, then brought her other knee onto his bed and framed his face with both hands. "I only know this," she whispered, leaning closer to cover his mouth with hers.

Gordon held his breath as she pulled him closer, stroking his lips with her tongue until he growled and wrapped his arms around her to tug her down on top of him.

She was soft and warm and Taylor. Sunshine and all things wonderful. Gordon lost himself in their kiss, tasting her singular, compelling flavor, savoring the molten flare of his blood.

Her slight weight pressed against him, erotic and tantalizing. He deepened the kiss, glorying in the feel of her tongue stroking his. Easing his hand along her rib cage, he found the fullness of her breast beneath the thin cotton of the T-shirt between them.

A tremor surged through him, but he held himself

in check, pulled back just short of his point of no return. She'd come here to apologize—not necessarily to make love. Breaking their kiss, he brought his hands to her face and stared into her eyes. He should hate her. He should fight this.

He couldn't.

"Taylor," he whispered, surrendering to the tumult of desire that banished every logical thought he'd strived so hard to maintain. "I've wanted you every day of my life. I want you *now.*"

Her nostrils flared slightly and a slow, sexy smile parted her lips. "How much?"

He flashed her a grin and pressed his hips against hers. "That much."

She licked her lower lip as he lifted the corner of his comforter in invitation, and she slithered beneath it and against him.

Reckless, wanton hunger flared in Taylor's belly. She wanted Gordon. Needed his gentleness.

"You're beautiful," he murmured, kissing her tenderly. In that suspended moment, she surrendered. Denying this was futile, regardless of the consequences. Coming into his room tonight had been the hardest thing she'd ever done, but also the most irresistible.

This moment was sacred—not something to be taken lightly. A hush of anticipation dawned as he lifted his face to meet her gaze for a few precious seconds. What was the emotion she saw blazing in his eyes? It made her stomach knot and her breath become imprisoned in her throat as she drowned in his gaze.

She was hot—hotter than she'd ever been. She coiled into a tight, rigid sprocket of expectation. Her breasts ached for more of his touch.

He slipped the T-shirt over her head and rolled her onto her back as he kissed each newly exposed portion of skin. Gently, he lowered his head to tickle the plain between her breasts with his tongue, making her groan in contemplation of more. Much more.

Hovering over her, he stroked the curve of her thigh, sensuously easing his hand farther down. She quivered against him, glorying in the feel of his warm skin against hers.

"Are you a dream?" he whispered.

"Whatever you do, don't wake me," she breathed, imprisoned by the intensity of his gaze.

Poised over her for a moment of sheer torture, he continued to stare. With trembling hands, she reached out to touch the taut, warm skin of his bare chest.

He pulled her against him, his furred chest tickling her upthrust nipples. His erection pressed insistently against her hip, making her clench against the agonizing emptiness of her womb. She wanted him. All of him. And she couldn't help but notice that ten years had made a significant difference in many things.

Yes, Gordon Lane had grown up in *every* way.

Taylor willed all reservations away as passion grew, possessed, and controlled her every thought and action. He ran his tantalizing fingers along her upper arms, then spread his hands flat against her rib cage.

He lightly stroked her waist and hips, bending to kiss the curve of her shoulder.

This was the Gordon she remembered. He worshiped her as he loved her, making each caress, each kiss, even more potent. More delicious.

Tracing circles around his flat nipple with her tongue, she felt it harden to a tiny nub. She stroked and kneaded his lower back, moving downward until his muscular butt seared the palms of her hands.

He growled low in his throat and pressed the evidence of his arousal against her hip more firmly. A physical pain of desire gripped her with a need so profound that she nearly wept from its intensity.

His lips covered hers as he took her face between his large hands almost savagely, tipping her head back as his tongue thrust into her mouth. She returned his passionate kiss, savored and cherished it, spiraling toward a pit of rapture like nothing she'd ever known before.

Even with Gordon. This was different from the fumbling, exploratory lovemaking of their youth. They were adults who knew what they wanted and how to give and take.

And this was so much more than sex. Taylor's heart filled her chest with joy and an exquisite ache. God, how she loved this man. What a fool she'd been. So many lost years . . .

But now was what mattered. She didn't care if this was right or wrong—and how could it be anything but right? She embraced this joy in the midst of all the pain and confusion. Gordon was strong and loving and gentle. She needed this. Needed *him*.

He withdrew his mouth from hers, lingered above her to stare for a long, silent moment. His hands touched her belly, then fanned upward to tease the tender undersides of her breasts. An untamed, primal yearning pounded a constant cadence in her body. She curled her legs around his and pulled him against her.

"Too soon," he murmured, obviously intent on torture with his dallying.

He kissed his way downward. His whiskered chin scraped against her ultrasensitive breasts until his lips opened moist and feverish to taste her nipple. First he teased, then he suckled firmly until she moaned aloud from the wonder of it all.

He eased one hand down her hip and pressed against the hard mound where her curling dark hair began. She gasped in anticipation and need.

Wrapping her arms around his neck, she clutched his mouth to her breast as his hand slipped between her thighs to explore her most intimate region. He toyed with her, creating a desperate need for more. She felt swollen yet empty until his fingers finally filled her, making her press and arch against him.

Memories fueled her. Other times. Other places. Other moments. The waterfall—their first time. The backseat of his old Jeep. Each time miraculous. Each time an exquisite pearl of a memory she had cherished every day since.

Hungry to relive those moments, she held her breath in anticipation, the need to touch him overpowering her. He gasped as her fingers closed around his smooth, hot erection.

"Easy," he muttered, dragging his mouth from her breast to gaze into her eyes.

His eyes—and other parts of his anatomy—were filled with promise. Taylor's breath caught in her throat as she ran her fingers over his swollen, pulsing manhood. He was so engorged, her fingers couldn't completely close around him.

Gordon kissed her again while his fingers continued to dominate her fevered flesh. She moaned and writhed against him, maintaining her grip on his erection as he urged her higher and higher in her crusade for completion.

He left her lips to kiss his way downward again, tarrying to impart equal treatment to both her breasts, licking the sensitive peaks—one, then the other—until Taylor thought she'd go mad. "Please, Gordon. Now."

Chuckling, he kissed his way lower, finally displacing his hand with his hot, seeking mouth. She gasped when his fingers again filled her while his mouth claimed the most sensitive part of her with maddening tenacity. Blackness surrounded her as he took her closer and closer to a pinnacle of joy she wanted so much that she felt like screaming.

When at last she exploded, thrusting herself against his warm, wonderful mouth, she separated from her body. She became a billion minuscule fragments floating lingeringly back to earth, each particle stunned, filled with a perfect contentment.

Though even in that moment of bliss, she knew there was more. Much more.

Growling, Gordon slid back up her body. She

wrapped her legs around his hips, pulling him closer. A hunger like nothing she'd ever imagined coiled inside her, making her arch and moan.

Finally, he pressed himself against her, and she opened like a flower to the sun, starving for full possession and the fulfillment he promised. "Gordon," she whimpered, and was rewarded with a guttural and supremely sexual sound from deep in his chest as he filled her.

Full. Complete. Whole. She didn't breathe for several seconds as she reveled in the wonder of their union. She'd never felt so complete. This was so right. So perfect. She wriggled against him, trying to take even more of him into her.

He froze above her. "Be still," he warned in a raspy voice. "I want this to last. Forever."

*Forever.* Murmuring her agreement against his chest, she tried to keep from moving, but her body seemed intent on following its natural instincts. She constricted around him—couldn't get enough of him.

He moved against her at last and she gasped with wonder. Angling her hips, she met him thrust for thrust—savored each glorious moment as she spiraled ever upward. This man was Gordon. *Her* Gordon.

An inferno built within her, so powerful, so all-encompassing, it could not burn itself out. Only the man who'd set the blaze could extinguish it.

She bit her lower lip as he moved faster and harder. Her body swallowed and accommodated his with a voraciousness that stunned her. She rose higher and higher until she exploded beneath and around him. Her face felt numb and tingly as all her blood rushed to fulfill nature's most powerful sensation.

He tensed against her, and she felt him throb and pulse with life as he came into her. A perverse sense of power washed through her and she clung to him in pure, uninhibited, carnal bliss.

The desire to possess Gordon Lane again had been more powerful than anything she'd ever felt in her entire life. Even more devastating than the urge to run away all those years ago. She kissed his sweat-slick shoulder.

"Taylor . . ." His voice was low and husky as he drew a ragged breath and released it into her hair. "Taylor."

He rolled to his side and ran his hand along the curve of her hip. "I . . . I . . ."

"Shh." She pressed a finger to his lips. "This was something we couldn't have prevented if we'd tried." She smiled slowly. "And I'm very glad it happened."

Gordon gazed into her eyes. She saw a hint of hesitation in the aqua depths. She recognized it and wondered about its source.

"What's wrong?" she asked, then wished she hadn't. Nothing should be permitted to decimate this moment. It was too perfect. *Was . . .*

"I'm sorry." He shook his head. "I have condoms in the nightstand, but . . ." With a sigh, he pulled her against him and kissed the top of her head. "I couldn't think of anything but being with you again."

"Neither of us thought." She stroked the fine hairs at his nape. "Just like our first time."

He raised up and gazed down at her, a gentle smile curving his full mouth. "Better."

"Mmm, I think you've learned a few tricks since then," she whispered, "but I've never forgotten that day. I never will."

"Nor will I."

"You're a beautiful man, Gordon Lane."

"Nobody's ever called me beautiful before." He pulled back to scowl at her in mock indignation. "Handsome, maybe, but definitely not beautiful."

"All of those things. Handsome, beautiful, and—" She bit her lower lip. She'd been about to say "mine." The thought that something so important could come so easily to her lips was terrifying. "I'm sorry."

"For what?" He gently kissed her lips, then raised himself up again. The glow from the oil lamp cast shadows of light and dark across the planes and angles of his handsome face. "For making love with me?"

"With me," Taylor repeated, warming within. "I like that."

"It's true." His smile lit his eyes. "Only you. Always you."

She tilted her head to one side to gaze into his eyes. Even if she should feel ashamed of the wild abandon she'd shown her lover, she didn't.

Gordon ran his fingers through his hair and chuckled. "You've become a hellcat in your old age." He gave her a crooked grin when she gasped out loud. "It's true."

Taylor stuttered and felt her face flood with heat. "Hellcat?" She was stunned yet flattered. "I'm . . . I'm sorry. I . . . I had no idea."

"*Sorry?* Definitely do *not* be sorry. It was the best—the very best," he vowed; then his expression grew solemn. "Everything I remembered . . . and so much more."

"Oh, Gordon." Words burned in her heart, begging to be released. "I'm so sorry I left. So very, very sorry. Can you ever forgive me?"

"You're back now," he murmured, kissing her again. "That's all that matters."

Her stomach lurched. Didn't he realize that she couldn't stay in Digby? That she had a life and a career waiting for her beyond this small mountain town?

"With your permission and participation," he whispered, "I'd like to find out if the next time can be as incredible as this one was."

"Next time?" She pushed aside thoughts of the future. So she was a hellcat in bed. Taylor-Pollyanna-Bowen? What a surprise. A giggle bubbled up from her chest as his mouth dipped to draw her nipple deep inside, making her laughter seize in her throat. "Gordon," she said quietly, gasping as his teeth grazed the tender nub.

"Something tells me this time will be even better," she whispered, closing her eyes for a moment of total bliss.

Rumbling low in his chest, Gordon lifted his face from her breast to cast her a look of promise and challenge all blended into one pithy glance. Then he pulled her to him and rolled with her until she sat astride his muscular form.

"I guarantee it," he promised in a rough voice,

cupping both her breasts in his large hands while she leaned forward to meet his insatiable mouth.

Groaning, he propped himself on more pillows. Taylor followed his lead, savoring the feel of his teeth and lips on her tender nipples as he tasted one, then the other.

"Yes, even better." She arched her hips against him, realizing how very ready he was when his erection pulsated against her.

He reached into the nightstand and retrieved a square packet, ripping it open with his teeth. A moment later, he was pressing against her again.

Repositioning herself, she lifted her hips above him until she felt his heavy, throbbing manhood probing her softness. Hard to soft—man to woman. It was an ancient communication of him soliciting entrance and her granting it.

A sense of power filled her as she pressed herself downward, enclosing him with a voraciousness that left her dazed. He moaned beneath her, obviously as stunned as she. Moving slowly against him, she tingled from head to toe as he continued his assault on her aching breasts. They felt heavy and swollen. She braced herself against the headboard and glanced down, noticing her rigid nipples seemed to have doubled in size. She couldn't resist the urge to watch his mouth cover and stroke her delicate flesh, making her insides contort, closing around his erection with even greater urgency.

She'd heard of people who got their thrills from watching themselves with mirrored ceilings and such, but she'd never experienced anything quite like this

before. Actually seeing his mouth open, then fuse to
her breast, made Taylor melt inside. It was so right—
so stimulating. He seemed to belong with her . . .
touching her.

Was Gordon Lane still her destiny?

Joy spawned deep in her core and spread through-
out her. She became taut and anxious as she neared
her completion, continuing to engage and press
against his thrusting pelvis.

Growling again, Gordon pressed himself upward
and felt her response. He held his breath, hoping to
prolong the exquisiteness of being buried deep
within this beautiful woman. Taylor. His Taylor.

She was so responsive, it was downright dangerous.

But what a way for a man to go.

Slowly, rhythmically, he pressed upward, matching
her movements, gasping each time her muscles con-
torted around him, as if to drain him of everything
he had. This woman was definitely a hellcat in bed.
He vividly remembered her adolescent passion but
had never suspected anything quite like this. She was
made for loving. Made for him.

Dangerous thoughts. He buried them as physical
needs overpowered everything else like a volcano
building to an eruption greater than any he'd ever
known before, even more powerful than their very
first time. Taylor had ignited something in him long
ago, and now the flames fanned hotter and brighter
than ever before. *Terrifying.*

*Fan-damn-tastic.*

Climbing, soaring higher with every plunge into
her receptive body, Gordon knew he was lost. This

woman had touched him right where it troubled most and comforted best. There was no doubt—his wound was mortal.

His Taylor was home. Home at last.

She cried out against him, leaning forward to sink her teeth gently into his shoulder. Elation filled him as he felt her contract around him. No longer struggling to hold himself back, he felt the pressure build. Her feminine muscles swallowed him tighter and deeper with her orgasm, claiming and devouring him as he clenched his teeth and drove upward and into her.

Finally, devastatingly, he burst within her. Like a land mine that had lain silent since Taylor's departure, he'd finally found the trigger to release his pent-up power. Only Taylor. There was no holding back. This was all-out surrender.

He was in deep trouble.

Taylor clung to him, wept against his shoulder. Sweat formed between them as his throbbing subsided, followed by her sigh of contentment that he shared tenfold.

He groaned, releasing her soft breasts as she tightened around him again in a sexual vise that made him want to shout. He'd never experienced anything like this before. Taylor was hot and sweet.

Like only Taylor *could* be.

She was everything rolled into one very neat little package. A surge of emotions threatened to evolve into words, but he bit the inside of his cheek to silence them. She slumped against him, showering him with little kisses.

He couldn't let her go again.

# THIRTEEN

Sue managed to reschedule all of Taylor and Gordon's appointments for the following week, and arranged for a doctor and a vet in Buena Vista to be on-call for human and animal emergencies. She was on a roll. With any luck at all, Gordon and Taylor were having a wonderful romantic interlude.

During the full moon.

She crossed fingers on both hands for a second, then decided to catch up on her filing while the office was so quiet. The phone rang and she answered on the first ring.

"Sue, it's Priscilla."

"Hi. Is Ryan giving you fits already?" School was closed today because of the storm, and Priscilla Lane was watching Ryan. He'd be out for the summer in two weeks. "Did he bring that mutt with him again? I told him—"

"No, no, it isn't that." The older woman's voice sounded worried. "He ran home to get a video game for this Play Station Gordon set up over here."

Gordon was spoiling Ryan. Sue would have to speak to him about that. "All right."

"He hasn't come back, Sue, and it's still pouring rain."

"Maybe he decided to wait out this latest downpour." Sue worried her lower lip even as she tried to justify Ryan's tardiness. "Did you call the house?"

"Yes, and there was no answer."

"Nobody's here today, so I'll go track him down." Ryan was barely ten—old enough to move around this small town unsupervised, but young enough for his mother to worry. "I'll call you as soon as I find him."

"And I'll call your house if he shows up here. You know, now that I think about it, he got real quiet after I mentioned Taylor and Gordon being stranded at his cabin."

"Oh?" Sue rubbed her temple, wondering why that information would bother Ryan. Of course, her son thought of Gordon like a father. "Oh, no, I hope he didn't—"

"I'm sure Ryan wouldn't do anything foolish, dear," Priscilla said. "I'll call your house if he turns up back here."

"Leave a message. Thanks."

Sue hung up the phone and grabbed her purse and umbrella just as the cat bells sounded. *Let it be Ryan,* she thought, then looked up and saw Jeremy Cole's smiling face. Another man stood behind him, dripping on the waiting room floor.

"Jeremy." She warmed with pleasure at seeing him. "You're a day early."

"I hope that's all right." He gave her a sheepish grin and a shrug. "I wanted to see you again. I've been making some plans I wanted to discuss with you."

Sue's heart skipped a beat, though she made certain her curiosity didn't show. At least, she sure as hell hoped it didn't. Love at first sight was impractical and downright foolish, but where Jeremy Cole was concerned, she couldn't help herself. She was madly, head-over-heels, hopelessly in love.

"Sue Wheeler, is that you?" The other man stepped around Jeremy and stared at her with wide hazel eyes. "I don't believe it's really you, all grown up."

Salt-and-pepper hair, mustache, something about his eyes . . . Sue squinted and shook her head. "I have a terrible memory. Can you enlighten me, please?"

"You don't remember?" The man held his hand against his chest and sighed. "I'm crushed, Red."

*Red?* Gasping in recognition, she hurried around the desk and threw her arms around Taylor's big brother. "Mike, is it really you? With that caterpillar under your nose and all that gray hair, I wasn't sure."

He kissed her cheek and held her at arm's length. "The one and only. Taylor gave Jeremy here my number, and I decided to come up for a visit while my wife and kids are visiting her parents in Texas. Speaking of my kid sister, where is she?"

Sue stood back and stared in wonder at Mike Bowen. She hadn't seen him since he'd come back from college for Taylor's graduation. After that, the Bowens had moved to Florida, and Taylor . . . Well, that was history. They were friends again now.

"I went by the house, but she wasn't home," Mike continued. "She here?"

"No, she went up to Gordon's place and there was a mud slide."

"She's all right?" Mike's eyes darkened.

"Fine. She's with Gordon."

In unison, he and Jeremy both said, "Oh?"

Sue's cheeks warmed and she wondered if Jeremy was really over Taylor. That would be just her luck.

"I gather there's some history between those two," Jeremy said thoughtfully.

"Oh, yeah, big time," Mike said, rolling his eyes. "Taylor never would talk about why she left home so suddenly, and she wouldn't listen when Mom tried to talk to her about Gordon later." He shrugged and met Sue's gaze. "They on again?"

Sue shot Jeremy a questioning look, then sighed. "I . . . I'm not sure, but I hope so."

Jeremy gave her a nod so slight she thought for a moment she might have imagined it. "I wish Taylor only happiness," he said.

Relieved, Sue smiled at both men. "I have a missing son to track down."

"Missing?" Jeremy grabbed her arm.

Quickly, Sue explained the situation, trying to make light of it, though her worry was growing.

"We'll help you look for him," Mike said. "I didn't know you had kids, Sue."

She smiled. "One ornery ten-year-old boy who's going to be in deep doo-doo if he doesn't turn up quick."

Jeremy slid his arm around her shoulders and

gave her a squeeze. "Ryan's lucky to have you for a mom." He kissed her cheek. "Let's go find the little urchin."

Sue met Mike's gaze and he winked at her. What was it about his eyes . . . ?

Jeremy and Mike had driven up in Mike's Toyota Land Cruiser, anticipating bad weather. Much better than a BMW, Sue decided, and she really liked this side of Jeremy. He'd thoroughly embraced Colorado casual and seemed totally at ease now in Digby.

And with her.

They went to Priscilla's house first, but she still hadn't heard from or seen Ryan. Worried, Sue gave Mike directions to her house, which was eerily silent, meaning Patches wasn't there either. On a hunch, she went to the kitchen to check the dry marker board she and Ryan used to leave messages for each other.

"Aha," she said, turning on the light so she could read her son's printing. "Oh, no."

"What is it?" Jeremy stood beside her and read the message. "He went to Gordon's. How far is that?"

"It isn't far, but there was a mud slide. The road's blocked."

Mike frowned. "We'll find him, Sue," he said. "Don't worry."

"Can we rent horses like we did last weekend?" Jeremy asked, going for the phone book on the counter. "Is Gordon's place accessible that way?"

"Yes, and if Ryan is on his mountain bike, he'd probably take that trail anyway."

Mike went to the window. "The rain's stopped and

it looks like the clouds are breaking up. I'm going to call the sheriff about Ryan. Do you have a recent picture, just in case?"

*Just in case . . .* "Everybody knows Ryan. This is a small town."

"I'm sorry."

She swallowed the lump in her throat as he turned around with a sober expression. His eyes bored into her. She'd known Mike Bowen all her life, but for some reason his eyes haunted her now. Why?

"Someone should stay here in case Ryan comes home," she said. "And let Priscilla know what's going on."

"I'll do that, if you're sure you don't need me to come along," Mike said.

"Thanks, Mike, but I'd like you to stay here." She faced Jeremy. "I'll get changed while you call the stable, and I'll get Mike a picture of Ryan, since he hasn't met him."

"If they don't have horses to rent today, I'll buy the whole stable," Jeremy vowed.

She smiled and raced up the stairs, praying her son was safe. He was all she had. She couldn't bear to lose Ryan.

In her room, she grabbed jeans, a wool sweater, hiking boots—typical high country attire. Mike and Jeremy had perfect timing. As she bent to tie her hiking boots, her gaze fell on Ryan's most recent school picture sitting on her dresser. His hazel eyes were fringed by sooty lashes, much darker than his red hair.

Sue rose and picked up the framed portrait for

Mike and swallowed hard. Ryan's eyes . . . She blinked.

No, it couldn't be.


Gordon stretched and yawned, then grew suddenly conscious of the soft, warm body curled up against his side. Memories bombarded him and he looked down at Taylor's head, resting against his shoulder.

The comforter slipped off her creamy shoulder and his breath caught. She was so soft, so warm, so . . . naked. So Taylor.

His male anatomy sprang to attention and he stroked the smooth slope of her shoulder along the edge of the blanket, down to the swell of her half-exposed breast. Watery sunlight slanted through the shutters, bathing her in gold. A fierce, sweet ache unfolded in his chest and he held her to him more tightly, kissing the top of her head.

Taylor was home.

Overcome with the enormity of having the only woman he'd ever loved in his arms, in his bed, and in his life again, he sighed. Forgiveness was a good thing, he decided, smiling when she wrinkled her face and opened her eyes.

Surprise registered in her eyes; then she blinked several times and a slow, sexy smile spread across her face. " 'Morning," she said huskily.

" 'Morning." He cupped her chin and kissed her soundly. She arched against him, all warm and sleepy and soft.

"Sun's coming out," he said as their kiss ended. "Remember the waterfall?"

Her eyes brightened and she nodded. "Always."

"It's not a far hike from here."

"I'd like that," she said quietly. "A lot. We could pack a picnic."

She started to push back the comforter, but Gordon chuckled and rolled over to pin her playfully to the bed. "Not so fast. We have all day, thanks to that mud slide."

"Mmm. Even better."

Well over an hour later, Taylor stepped out into the rain-kissed air with Gordon. Max darted past them, but Gordon called the old dog back.

"Not this time, fella." He scratched the setter behind the ears and put him back inside with the promise of a good run tomorrow.

They walked in silence to the crest of the hill behind Gordon's cabin, where the terrain began to look familiar to Taylor. She held her breath, gazing down at the little canyon where the rain-swollen creek spilled down. "Silas Canyon?"

"Yep." Gordon pulled her into his arms and kissed her, making her shiver in anticipation of what they'd once shared in that very canyon.

Their first time. So long ago, but as vivid in her memory as if it had been yesterday. In a way, yesterday had been like a first time all over again.

"I want to make love with you behind the falls again," he murmured against her lips.

Desire shot through her, sure and sweet. "Yes," she breathed, not caring that the early June air was far cooler than it had been on that unforgettable Fourth of July.

He adjusted the backpack containing their picnic lunch and a bottle of wine, then took her hand. Taylor stared at his hand for several moments, then placed hers in his. Their gazes met and her heart must've stopped beating. Then he squeezed her hand and they began their trek together down into Silas Canyon to face the past.

And the future?

"Tell me about the medical research you want to do," he said as they made their way down the twisting trail.

She told him about her mother's asthma and allergies, and how she wanted to help others with that problem. Talking about it reminded her that medical research was something she'd never be able to do in Digby. She glanced askance at Gordon and forbid herself to think of anything but here and now.

And him.

They didn't have Henrietta along this time, but Taylor recognized the spot where Gordon had parked his Jeep that warm summer afternoon. She walked right to it and stopped, gazing up into his eyes. "Here?"

He nodded, his expression intense. "You remember."

"Always," she repeated.

Gordon pointed toward the falls. The sun was warm on their bare heads and faces, but the water would be frigid this early in the season. Actually, the water was always frigid in the high country. She smiled, remembering again.

He headed toward the falls without releasing Taylor's hand, but she stopped suddenly and pulled free. "Hey, this isn't how it happened."

His brow furrowed, he gave her a quizzical look. "No, not exactly."

Taylor bit her lower lip and looked around. Could she? *Hell, why not?* She unbuckled her fanny pack and let it slide to the ground, then bent to untie her hiking boots and kicked them off, too.

Straightening, she met Gordon's gaze. He devoured and caressed her with his eyes, his nostrils slightly flared, a thin film of perspiration beading his brow.

"Get with the program, Doctor," she said, unzipping her jeans and wriggling until they joined the growing pile near her feet.

"Holy . . ." Gordon drew a sharp breath as she reached for the hem of the sweater she'd borrowed from him and peeled it over her head.

Taylor had gone braless deliberately, savoring the decadent feel of angora against her bare nipples. Gordon's caressing gaze seemed to approve.

"You're beautiful," he said reverently.

Taylor flashed him a mischievous grin and hooked her thumbs in the waistband of her plain white panties. "You planning to get naked or not?" she quipped, earning a smile from him in turn.

"Did I mention the fancy cabin someone built overlooking the—"

Taylor grabbed the sweater and clutched it to her bare breasts. "Are you *serious?*"

Laughing, he said, "Yeah, but they're only around in August and during the holidays." He pointed at the sweater in her hands. "Drop it, or I don't shed a stitch."

She threw it at him. "Better?"

"Oh, yeah." He slid the backpack from his shoulders and loosened his belt, then popped the snap at his waistband. After kicking off his boots without taking his eyes off her, he eased the zipper down, then slipped off his jeans.

His boxers did little to conceal the evidence of his desire. *What's up, Doc?* Taylor's mouth went dry and heat pooled low in her belly. Anticipation oozed through her.

He stood there in the sunshine wearing nothing but his boxer shorts, reminding her of the day she'd returned to Digby. She should've known then that this would happen.

Fate. Inevitable.

He bent down and gathered their discarded clothing and tucked it under his arm, then slung his backpack over one shoulder and took her hand. "Shall we?"

His gaze lingered on the swell of her breasts and she could barely breathe. She wanted him so much it hurt, but what a sweet, sweet ache.

"You ran last time," he said with a grin.

"Mmm, I'm older now." She smiled and squeezed his hand. "You don't have to chase me."

"Damn. I was looking forward to watching everything . . . jiggle."

Taylor laughed and did a little shimmy, savoring the heat of his gaze. "Satisfied?"

"Hardly."

Her gaze dropped to the prominent tent at the front of his boxers. "Yes, I can see that."

He laughed again and she warmed at the sound. Having Gordon in her life again meant more to her than she'd imagined it could. If only she could find a way to have him and her career. . . .

*Stop it, Taylor.* Now wasn't the time to think about that. Concentrating on this moment, she watched him place their clothes on a sunny ledge far from the waterfall's spray.

"No bears around, I hope," she said nervously, remembering the last time she'd found Gordon here.

"Don't worry. You're safe with me." His expression and tone grew solemn. "I won't let a bear or anything else hurt you."

"I know that." She smiled up at him again, transported back to that warm Fourth of July between their junior and senior years in high school. . . .

Gordon set his backpack against the back wall, as far from the falls as possible, then opened it and removed something. As he turned to face her, holding a faded Indiana Jones beach towel in his hands, remembrance surged to the forefront of her mind.

His expression intense and adoring, he stepped closer and unfolded the towel, then spread it gently on the smooth stone slab at their feet. Taylor looked down at the faded image of Harrison Ford . . . and remembered.

Realization made her dizzy and tears sprang to her eyes. The memory of the day she'd given her virginity to him rose up between them, as special and powerful now as then. He'd kept the beach towel all this time. No ordinary man would've done something like this, but Gordon was extraordinary. Special. She realized that more and more with each passing day.

He held his arms out to her, seeming suddenly, and endearingly, shy. Taylor walked into the protective circle of his embrace, surrounded by the special, gentle love that only this man could give her. "Love me, Gordon," she whispered.

"Always."

And he did.

Ryan parked his bike near Gordon's front porch and bent down to pet Patches. The dog was panting heavily, his tongue hanging out one side of his mouth. Ryan bent closer. No wheezing.

Relieved, he straightened and looked around. No sign of anyone, but there were two Jeeps and Dr. Bowen's car parked in front of the cabin. With a sigh, Ryan went to the door and knocked. No answer. He knocked again and listened, hearing only Max inside, scratching at the door and whimpering.

"Hey, Max, it's just me," Ryan said. Patches growled. "Oh, lighten up, Patch."

Ryan decided to decorate Gordon's yard—especially around Dr. Bowen's car—with tracks, then head back down the mountain before they returned. They'd obviously gone for a hike, since all the cars were here and the road was still blocked. He glanced up at the sky. Clouds were gathering again. He'd better hurry.

He untied the track-maker from his handlebars and moved closer to the Volkswagen, but the ground was already covered with tracks. Bear tracks. The skin on the back of Ryan's neck felt all prickly, just like when his mom caught him doing something he knew he shouldn't.

"Hey, squirt," Gordon called from the far side of the cabin.

Holding his track-maker behind his back, Ryan whirled around to face Gordon and Dr. Bowen. "Hey, Gordon, that rowdy bear's been here again."

Gordon rolled his eyes and Dr. Bowen smiled.

And they were holding hands.

"Uh, see?" Ryan said, pointing at the ground in front of Dr. Bowen's car. "And over there, too." He indicated an area closer to the cabin.

"Give it up, Ryan." Gordon held out his hand. "Give me that gadget."

Ryan swallowed hard. "What gadget?"

"The one behind your back."

*Uh-oh.* Ryan had almost forgotten the track-maker. He brought it out from behind his back. "I didn't get a chance to use it yet," he said. "These are real tracks."

"Sure, Ryan," Dr. Bowen said. "Like the ones at my house?"

Ryan's face felt like it was on fire. "Uh . . ." H
gave a shrug and handed Gordon his track-maker
"But these are real."

"Have you heard the story of the boy who crie
wolf, Ryan?" Gordon asked in a stern voice. "You'v
cried bear one time too many."

Ryan couldn't stand for Gordon to be mad at him
"I . . . I . . ."

"Why, Ryan?" Dr. Bowen came closer and stoo
in front of Ryan. "What did I ever do to make yo
want to frighten me?"

Ryan clenched his teeth and lifted his chin
notch. He'd talk to Gordon, but not to *her.*

"Go ahead and be stubborn." Gordon shrugge
and handed the track-maker back to Ryan. "Retir
this thing and try being honest for a change."

Anger flared in Ryan's belly and he wanted t
strike out or cry or say those words his mother didn'
like him to use. But he didn't. It hurt too much t
have the man he wanted as his father look at hin
that way.

"I'm sorry," he muttered.

Dr. Bowen put her hand on Ryan's shoulder an
kissed his cheek. He scrubbed it viciously as sh
stepped away. Laughing.

"Why'd you go and do a fool thing like that for?"

Gordon chuckled and said, "Someday you'll ap
preciate it when a beautiful woman kisses you, pal.

"I doubt it." Ryan kept rubbing his cheek. "Girl
got cooties."

Dr. Bowen and Gordon both laughed; then Gor
don said, "We'd better see if the phone's workin

yet so we can call your mom and let her know you're okay."

"I left her a note."

"Yeah, and I'm sure finding a note saying you went up the mountain alone after a mud slide gives her a warm, fuzzy feeling." Gordon arched a brow. "Hmm?"

"Yeah, we better call her." Ryan hadn't meant to worry his mom or make Gordon mad or anything. He'd only wanted to . . . to . . . He looked at Dr. Bowen again while Gordon fumbled in his pocket for his keys. Why'd she have to be so doggone nice? He sighed and leaned on the track-maker. "I really am sorry."

"You're forgiven," she said.

"Well, looks like I lost my keys." Gordon kept digging through both pockets. "Mom and Sue have the spares."

"They must've fallen out of your pocket when you took off—uh, back in Silas Canyon." Dr. Bowen's face turned fire-engine red.

"Hmm." Gordon glanced up. "And it's going to rain again. Too bad Max can't unlock the door. Guess I'll have to break a win—"

A low and uncaninelike growl rumbled from the side of the cabin. Patches bolted for the source of the growl. Ryan ran after his dog, but Dr. Bowen grabbed Ryan.

Gordon threw open the door to his old Jeep. "Get in."

"Patches," Ryan called as Dr. Bowen and Gordon

both hauled him toward the Jeep. The dumb dog disappeared around the corner. *"Patches!"*

Another growl and a high-pitched yelp preceded the dog's speedy return. They all piled into the Jeep together—Gordon and Taylor in front, Patches and Ryan in back.

Breathing hard, they watched the bear lumber around to the front porch, sniffing the ground and making low rumbling sounds. The bear paused at Ryan's bike and nudged it with its nose, then turned toward Henrietta.

Taylor squeaked, and Gordon put his arm around her shoulders. Disgusted, Ryan closed his eyes and released a heavy sigh.

"We're safe in here," Gordon said quietly, rubbing her neck and shoulders. "Don't worry."

Ryan folded his arms across his rumbling belly. "Got anything to eat?"

Gordon chuckled. "Cheese and wine in my backpack."

"Wine?" Ryan's hopes soared. He'd tasted wine once when Mrs. Lane wasn't watching her evening glass too closely.

"Not for you, squirt," Gordon said, pointing toward the front porch. "Besides, my backpack's over there."

The Jeep moved, and Ryan saw the bear's head appear over the hood as it stared through the windshield at them. Dr. Bowen buried her face against Gordon's shoulder.

"Man, this sucks."

"Watch your language, young man," Gordon said

and honked the horn. The bear dropped down to all fours and returned to the porch.

"A bear. A *real* bear," Dr. Bowen said.

"He's out there and we're in here, Taylor." Gordon pulled her closer, and Ryan kept his thoughts to himself.

"Well, so much for the cheese and wine," Dr. Bowen said as she looked up with a nervous laugh. "Maybe he'll get drunk and pass out."

"I'll bet he's a *she,*" Ryan said, narrowing his gaze on the back of Dr. Bowen's head.

"Doesn't matter." Gordon pointed. "Well, there goes a perfectly good backpack."

Ryan saw that the bear had clawed open the whole side of the backpack and was pulling things out with its teeth. It paused to chew. "Must've found the cheese."

"I didn't know bears ate cheese," Dr. Bowen said, sounding calmer now that the bear was away from the Jeep.

"Bears eat just about anything." Gordon shrugged. "There goes the wine." The bottle rolled off the porch and broke, spilling red liquid across the bare ground. "Now maybe it'll finish up and get out of here."

Patches growled and barked at the closed window. "Hush," Ryan said.

The bear lumbered past the Jeep again, pausing to stare at the occupants, then headed toward the creek. "It's about time. I'll get us inside the cabin in no time." Gordon opened the door. "You two stay here until I get the front door open. Just in case."

"Not a problem," Dr. Bowen said.

Ryan didn't say a word. He'd much rather risk the bear than stay in here with Dr. Bowen. If she hadn't come here, Gordon might be ready to marry Mom. Resentment oozed through Ryan and he clenched his teeth.

"Look." Dr. Bowen pointed toward the woods across the clearing.

"Mom?" Ryan saw his mom and that nasty Dr. Dweeb emerging from the woods on horseback.

"She must've been very worried." Dr. Bowen looked back at Ryan, then waved to the newcomers.

Ryan watched his mom's horse rear. She fell and the horse bolted. "Mom!" He grabbed the door handle, but Dr. Bowen grabbed his arm.

"No, Ryan."

Frightened for his mother, Ryan looked out again and saw Dr. Cole's horse pawing the earth and snorting as he dismounted. Then Ryan saw the reason for the horses' fear.

That stupid bear again.

Dr. Bowen opened the window but didn't release her grip on Ryan's arm. "Hurry, this way."

The brave yuppie-dweeb scooped Mom up as if she didn't weigh a thing and ran to the Jeep. He opened the back door and slid in beside Ryan and Patches.

The dog growled.

"Sue, are you all right?" Dr. Cole pushed her hair back from her face.

He looked really worried about Mom.

His mom smiled. "I am now."

And she was sitting in that dumb doctor's lap with that silly, disgusting, lovesick look on her face. Ryan scooted closer to the door, almost ready to take his chances with the bear, who was now busy with Gordon's backpack again.

"Ryan Paul Wheeler," his mom said in that voice Ryan hated more than anything. "What possessed you to do something so . . . so . . . ?" She slid off Dr. Cole's lap and grabbed Ryan and Patches both in a bear hug.

*Bear hug. Yeah, right.* Ryan let his mom smother him with kisses, knowing in another minute she'd be yelling at him again. But at least she was off Dr. Dweeb's lap.

"Where's Gordon?" Dr. Bowen asked.

That distracted his mom for a minute. "What happened? Is he in the cabin?"

Dr. Bowen shook her head. "He lost his keys and we couldn't get in. Good thing Henrietta wasn't locked."

"I'll say," Dr. Dweeb said, pressing his forehead against the window to watch the bear. "The only bears I've ever seen were in the zoo."

"Unfortunately, I've seen too many," Dr. Bowen said in a weak voice. "I wish Gordon would come back."

"Where is he?" Ryan's mom asked again.

"Trying to break into the cabin."

"Huh." Mom shook her head. "I remember when

he built that thing. He said he wanted it to stand a thousand years. I don't think he *can* break in."

A moment later, Gordon appeared at the side of the cabin, peering at the bear. While it busied itself chewing something else from the destroyed backpack, Gordon made a dash for the Jeep and didn't stop until he was sitting in the driver's seat, huffing and puffing.

"Remind me never to build my own house a—" He jerked his head around to stare at the new arrivals. "How'd you two get here?"

"Horseback," Dr. Dweeb said, offering Gordon his hand. "We meet again."

"Dr. Cole." Gordon lifted both brows and shook Dr. Dweeb's hand.

"Jeremy, please."

"Fine, call me Gordon. Sue, I don't suppose you have my spare key with you?"

She shook her head and shrugged. "Sorry, but all I could think of was finding this juvenile delinquent here."

"Sheesh," Ryan said.

"I'm still waiting for an explanation about why you decided to scare me half to death by running off, Ryan," Mom said, reaching out to grab his track-maker and holding it up in front of her. "And I suppose you have a very good reason for this contraption."

Gordon and Dr. Bowen both stared at him expectantly.

He was in deep doo-doo.

\* \* \*

Taylor's heart ached for Ryan. She knew why he was trying to run her out of Digby. She met Gordon's gaze and he took her hand discreetly.

"Well, Ryan?" Sue prodded.

Ryan's face reddened and he doubled up his fist to smack his jeans-clad thigh. Then he mumbled something completely unintelligible.

"What was that?" Sue cupped her hand to her ear. "I didn't hear you."

" 'Cuz I want *you* to marry Gordon." Ryan turned to stare out the window. "That's all."

Patches put his front paws on the seat and licked the boy's ear. Ryan buried his face against the mutt and fell silent.

As did all the adults in the Jeep. Taylor looked from Sue to Gordon, then at a stunned Jeremy. What could they say? They'd asked Ryan for an explanation and he'd given it succinctly.

"Ryan," Sue said, touching her son's shoulder. "Gordon and I are friends. More like brother and sister after all these years."

Ryan remained silent with his face hidden in all that black-and-white fur.

"Your mom's right, Ryan," Gordon said, turning completely around in his seat. "Did you know I even asked her to marry me once, but she said no?"

Ryan lifted his face and sniffled, looking at Gordon. "You did?"

"Yep. She told me that'd be like marrying her own brother."

"Yuck," Sue said.

Ryan nodded. Apparently, that made sense to a

ten-year-old's perception of the world. "Yeah, I get it," he said, then turned to stare out the window. "I told Dr. Bowen I was sorry about trying to scare her."

"Yes, he did," Taylor said. "And I forgave him."

More strained silence spanned between them, and Taylor wished someone would say *something*.

"Well, now that *that's* settled," Jeremy said jovially, "I have a little announcement to make."

Taylor met Sue's curious gaze, but the other woman shook her head. Whatever Jeremy's announcement was, Sue obviously didn't know about it yet.

"Taylor, your brother told me while I was in Denver that he's found a research grant for you at Children's Hospital." He smiled. "In immunology."

A dull roar began in her ears. "What?" Her mouth turned dry and she tried to swallow the lump in her throat. She felt Gordon stiffen beside her, even though he'd dropped her hand when he turned around to speak to Ryan. "But I'm sure they won't wait three years for—"

"Ah, but that's where I come in," Jeremy said, still smiling. "I called the mayor and asked him if he'd take me in your stead."

The roar grew louder.

"You did *what?*" Sue asked. "You mean you *want* to stay in Digby?"

Ryan released a long sigh, which Patches echoed.

"More than anything," Jeremy continued. "And, Taylor, the mayor said yes. As soon as we get the contracts drawn up and signed, you're free to go to Denver."

"I see." Taylor couldn't bring herself to look at Gordon. After their incredible reunion, the last thing she wanted was to leave him. But what about her dream? This was a huge and incredible opportunity. How could she turn her back on this?

She glanced from Jeremy to Sue, realizing she had to agree. It was, after all, what she'd always wanted. Wasn't it?

And Sue and Jeremy belonged together. She smiled and drew a deep breath. "Well, I don't want to make any decision without talking to the folks at Children's Hospital first." That would buy her a little time.

"Yes, definitely." Sue squirmed, obviously uncomfortable with this discussion. "And I think Jeremy should think this over before—"

"I have thought it over." He took Sue's hand and held it in both of his. "I've done nothing but think about Digby." He smiled. "And you."

"Yuck," Ryan whispered, and all the adults chuckled nervously.

"You know, I believe that bear has taken a hike," Jeremy said.

Taylor turned to look at Gordon and her breath froze in her throat. The expression on his face ripped her heart out. He averted his gaze and reached for the door handle.

"I'll get that back door open this time," he said.

Then he was gone.

"I'm going, too." Ryan jerked open the door and scrambled out with Patches.

"Make lots of noise, Ryan," Sue called when her dive to stop her son failed. She looked at Taylor and shrugged. "Can you believe I'm telling him to make more noise than usual?"

Taylor gave a sad smile and met Jeremy's gaze. "Did I . . . screw up?" he asked.

She sighed and tilted her head to one side. "I . . . I'm just in a state of be careful what you wish for, Jeremy." She gave him another sad smile and Sue reached for her hand. "That's all."

"Well, I suppose I'll get out with the . . . men." Jeremy flashed a boyish grin and opened his door. He leaned over and gave Sue a peck on the cheek. "And I promise to make lots of noise."

The door closed and Taylor said, "My God, he's actually charming. What have you done to him?"

Sue laughed. "He's wonderful. Taylor, do you believe in love at first sight?"

Taylor squeezed Sue's hand and drew a deep breath. "If you'd asked me that question a month ago, I would've said no."

"Now?" Sue's eyes were wide and expectant.

"Now, seeing you and Jeremy, I have to say definitely yes."

Sue's hundred-watt smile illuminated the inside of the Jeep. "Thanks."

"You're very welcome." She sighed. "And thank you for making me talk to Gordon."

"Is everything okay now with you two?"

Taylor blinked back the tears stinging her eyes and

cleared her throat. "For just a little while, everything was perfect." She rubbed her aching forehead. "Absolutely perfect."

"Oh."

Jeremy returned to the Jeep and opened the door. Poking his head inside, he said, "It's all clear now and the front door's open, thanks to Ryan."

"Ryan?"

"Yeah, he fit through the basement window." Jeremy chuckled and held his hand out while Sue slid out of the backseat.

Taylor climbed from the Jeep and shivered. The sky was dark and brooding again like her mood, and she was no longer alone with Gordon. Even so, they were surrounded by good friends, and she had some important decisions to make. Being alone with Gordon would cloud her judgment.

She had to think with her head, not her heart.

# FOURTEEN

Gordon looked in the mirror in his office and straightened his tie. He'd be late for the wedding if he didn't leave right now. A soft knock on the door startled him. He didn't have time to deal with anything right now. Flustered, he opened the door and found Mike Bowen wearing a very serious expression.

"Mike, aren't you supposed to be at the church?"

"Yeah, but so are you." He inclined his head. "Got a minute?"

Gordon nodded. "Come on in. They can't start without us."

Mike sat in a chair across from Gordon's desk while he leaned on the edge of it with his arms folded across his abdomen.

"What's up?" Gordon asked.

"I was talking to Taylor last night," Mike said, "and she told me about . . ."

"Us?"

"No, but we're going to get to that in a minute, too." Mike grinned, then shook his head. "She told me about Ryan—about how Sue got . . ."

"Pregnant?" Gordon nodded. "Go on. I'm listening."

Mike gave a nervous laugh and raked his hands through his hair. "I came back from college for your graduation."

"Yeah, I remember."

"Sue was partying with me and Rick Miller that night."

"Are you saying Rick—"

"No, he would have taken responsibility. You know that." Mike shook his head, a stricken expression on his face. "It was me, Gordon. We were both plastered—dumb teenage stuff—and after Rick went home, Sue and me, we . . ." He rolled his eyes. "And *she* doesn't remember."

"Oh, God." Gordon released a breath and rubbed the back of his neck. "Man, I had no idea."

"And I didn't know she was pregnant." Mike stood and paced the room. "How could I have known? My family moved away. Taylor wouldn't talk about why she left, but the minute I heard the story of how Sue ended up pregnant . . ."

"You knew."

Mike nodded. "And how am I going to tell her?"

"You have a family now, Mike," Gordon said soberly. "Sue has a right to that, too, but she also has a right to the truth."

"Yes, and Ryan's my son." Mike's eyes flashed. "My *son*."

"Well, after Sue and Jeremy come back from their honeymoon, you'll have to tell them the truth, then let them decide how to tell Ryan."

Mike nodded. "I never would've let her do this alone if I'd known."

"Of course not." Gordon shoved away from the desk and patted Mike on the shoulder. "That means Ryan's about to get a stepdad, a birth dad, and an aunt." *Taylor.*

"And grandparents in Florida." Mike laughed again, then smiled. Really smiled. "They'll be thrilled."

"And your wife?"

Mike's expression sobered. "She'll be all right with this. We have a good marriage, and Sue happened a long time before I met her. Thanks, Gordon."

"Did your family drive up with you?" Gordon asked as they moved by mutual and silent consent toward the door.

"Yeah, they're at the church. Taylor drove up on her own." Mike paused outside and gave Gordon a questioning look. "She's miserable, you know."

*She's not the only one.* "This is her dream, Mike." He shook his head. No reason to be evasive with Mike. He knew how much Taylor meant to Gordon. "Loving her meant letting her go."

"Cut the noble shit," Mike said. "For once in your life, be selfish, Gordon. You're crazy about each other, and it's high time one of you stopped making sacrifices and decided to take what you want from life. You're a couple of frigging martyrs."

Taken aback, Gordon stared long and hard at Taylor's brother. "Yeah, you have a point, and I appreciate your advice," he said. "And I promise to think it over after the wedding. Honest."

"Taylor's staying up here to cover for Jeremy at the new clinic while they're honeymooning." Mike sighed and looked at his watch. "If we don't get a move on, Sue will kill us both and we won't have to worry about anything anymore."

Gordon chuckled and climbed into Henrietta to follow Mike across town to the church. Mike's lecture replayed itself through his head all through the ceremony.

He watched Ryan walk Sue down the aisle. The kid had decided that Jeremy wasn't half bad after learning that he could fish *and* ride a horse. Jeremy had even helped Taylor diagnose Patches' allergy to Ryan's down comforter, which explained why the dog's condition worsened with cooler weather. Some bird dog.

And, most important of all, as Ryan had announced in a very grown-up way, Dr. Dweeb made his mom smile.

*What could be more perfect?*

Gordon stood up as Jeremy's best man, but his gaze kept drifting beyond the bride and groom to Taylor. He caught her gaze once and held it for a lingering moment. She was the most beautiful maid of honor who'd ever lived, he decided.

After the service, he took her arm and followed the newlyweds back down the aisle. His mother surprised him by giving a thumbs-up signal as they passed. Priscilla Lane was in her glory, playing surrogate mother of the bride to the hilt, and entertaining Jeremy's disapproving blue-blood parents while they were in town. Had her thumbs-up gesture been because of the successful ceremony, or for Gordon and Taylor?

It felt wonderful to hold Taylor's arm close to his side. He'd missed her every minute of every day and night since she'd left Digby only a month ago. Thank goodness Sue and Jeremy's wedding and honeymoon had brought her back, even if it was only for two weeks.

*She's miserable, you know.*

God help him, so was he. Maybe Mike was right.


Taylor walked the Kenners to the waiting room of the Eddington Clinic after removing Adam's cast. The boy gave her a hug and a sticky kiss at the door. Tears clouded Taylor's vision for a moment, but she blinked them away.

"You be careful a while longer," she said, and gave his mother a reassuring smile. "No tree-climbing or bike-riding for at least a week."

Mrs. Kenner rolled her eyes and thanked Taylor, then left the clinic with her mended child. Envy spread through Taylor unbidden as she watched mother and son climb into the cab of a pickup truck. Would she ever have a child of her own?

With a sigh, she turned to see Jeremy's receptionist deftly handle another phone call. He'd hired Sally Bradshaw to run the office at the clinic, and she was doing a pretty decent job, too. Goldie lifted her head and blinked at Taylor, then resumed her nap.

"Got an emergency, Dr. Bowen," Sally said, feeling the edges of her memo pad with her fingers and tearing off a slip of paper. "Let me know if you can't read that, and I'll translate."

"You're a goddess, Sally." Taylor took the note and frowned. "Isn't this . . . ?"

"Yep, it's Gordon's cabin all right. No other houses out that way."

"Yeah, I know." Worry slithered through Taylor. The message read: *Matter of life and death—come at once.*

"That's it? What kind of emergency?" Taylor folded the note and put it in her pocket. "Was it Gordon who called?"

"Nooooo." Sally bit her lower lip. "I think it was Ryan."

"Ryan?" Priscilla was taking care of Ryan. Maybe the boy had gone to Gordon's cabin and had some kind of accident. Her nephew. Ryan.

"I'm gone. Hold down the fort."

"You know it." Sally waved as Taylor practically flew by her desk.

Taylor hurried to Jeremy's office, yanked off her lab coat, grabbed her bag, then raced out to her car. All the way up Gordon's mountain, her heart thundered to the cadence of her worry.

Either Gordon or Ryan was hurt. Ryan wouldn't have called for anything less.

Both Jeeps were parked in front of the cabin when she arrived, but no other vehicles. Taylor grabbed her bag and jumped from her car, then threw open the door to Gordon's cabin without bothering to knock.

He looked up from the ledger on his rolltop desk, his eyes widening in obvious surprise. "Taylor?"

"Where's Ryan?" she asked. "Is he hurt?"

Gordon rose, shaking his head. "Ryan isn't here." He frowned. "What made you think—"

The phone rang and he answered it. "Yeah, Taylor's here, Sally. Just a sec."

He held the phone out to her. "Your office."

She took the phone and said, "Dr. Bowen."

"I was instructed to give you the rest of the message after you got there," Sally said solemnly. "Are you ready, Doctor?"

Suspicious, Taylor watched Gordon's face as she listened to Sally. He looked totally innocent.

"Ryan said, 'Tell Dr. Bowen that Gordon is suffering from a broken heart and only she has the cure.'"

Taylor's throat felt very full. She cleared it and asked, "He did, huh?" Her lips twitched and she thanked Sally before hanging up the phone. "Ryan's quite a character."

"Runs in the family," Gordon said approvingly. "Both sides."

"Yeah, it does." She grinned. "He called in a medical emergency at your address."

"You're kidding?" Gordon took a step closer. "What kind of medical emergency?" His voice fell to a husky whisper.

"The most serious kind—a matter of life and death." She gave a dramatic sigh, though she felt more like crying and shouting and venting. "And I'm afraid I'm suffering from the same ailment."

"Taylor . . ." He paused in front of her, so close she felt his heat. "What is it?"

"A . . ." She bit her lower lip to still its tremor. "Ryan said you're suffering from a broken heart, and only I have the cure."

He flashed her a crooked grin. "That little squirt."

"Is one smart kid." She drew a shaky breath. "Gordon, I miss you."

Before she drew her next breath, she was in his arms. "I've missed you, too, and I was going to call you tonight," he murmured against her hair. Then he held her at arm's length and stared intently into her eyes. "I want to see your face when I tell you this."

Her heart stuttered, then plunged into overdrive. "What?"

"I *love* you, Taylor Bowen, with everything I have." He kissed her, then pulled away again. "You're part of me. You make me whole. I'm miserable without you."

Tears rolled unheeded down her cheeks and she cupped his face in her hands. "I love you, too, Gordon. So much." She trembled in his embrace. "And I promise you one thing—"

"You don't have to promise me anything, Taylor," he said. "Just love me."

"Oh, I do."

He pulled her closer and kissed her, long, slow, deep, committed. When they parted, he brushed her hair from her eyes. "You'll have your research, too. I swear it."

She nodded. "I can commute."

"I'm going to be teaching in Denver three days a week," he said, smiling. "We'll get a condo in the city and come up here weekends. I'll give the clinic here Fridays and Mondays, which is about all they need anyway."

"Gordon, that's wonderful." Her throat clogged with more tears and she shook her head. "It's perfect. You're perfect."

"No, I'm not perfect," he said quietly, "but I'm the man who loves you. Never forget that."

"And my promise is that I trust you as much as I love you." She watched his eyes brighten as she spoke. "I always will."

He whirled her around the cabin and jumped over a sleeping Max, and they ended up sprawled across Gordon's bed. "We should call Ryan and let him know his diagnosis was correct," Taylor said, stretching out to cover Gordon.

"Hmm, good idea. Besides, I have a job for him in the not-too-distant future."

"What's that?" She lifted her head to stare into the eyes of the man she loved.

"Have him use that bear track-maker of his to keep people away from this cabin during our honeymoon."

"Honeymoon?"

"Count on it." He gave her that bone-melting look again. "I'd say we're definitely a medical miracle, Doctor. A complete cure, in fact."

She smiled. "Only if ongoing treatment is applied liberally and often." She kissed him soundly.

He growled low in his throat and whispered, "Always."